NOT A GOOD SIGN

My first clue that something is very, very wrong is the giggling. It hits me like a wave of endorphins as I pull open the door to the Academy courtyard. Girls giggling. Lots of girls giggling. Lots of *young* girls giggling.

When I step into the open, I see them huddled in a little giggling mass around a bench in the far corner. There are at least a dozen of them. And they are all, like, *ten*.

I look desperately around the courtyard for signs of anyone who has successfully survived puberty. No. There is only me and the ten-year-olds.

My heart drops like a lead weight into my stomach. Nicole's uncontrollable laughter when she found out I was going to this stupid camp now makes total sense.

⚜⚜⚜⚜⚜⚜⚜⚜

OTHER BOOKS YOU MAY ENJOY

goddess boot camp

Tera Lynn Childs

speak

An Imprint of Penguin Group (USA) Inc.

SPEAK

Published by the Penguin Group

Penguin Group (USA) Inc., 345 Hudson Street, New York, New York 10014, U.S.A.

Penguin Group (Canada), 90 Eglinton Avenue East, Suite 700, Toronto, Ontario, Canada M4P 2Y3
(a division of Pearson Penguin Canada Inc.)

Penguin Books Ltd, 80 Strand, London WC2R 0RL, England

Penguin Ireland, 25 St Stephen's Green, Dublin 2, Ireland (a division of Penguin Books Ltd)

Penguin Group (Australia), 250 Camberwell Road, Camberwell, Victoria 3124, Australia
(a division of Pearson Australia Group Pty Ltd)

Penguin Books India Pvt Ltd, 11 Community Centre, Panchsheel Park, New Delhi - 110 017, India

Penguin Group (NZ), 67 Apollo Drive, Rosedale, North Shore 0632, New Zealand
(a division of Pearson New Zealand Ltd.)

Penguin Books (South Africa) (Pty) Ltd, 24 Sturdee Avenue,
Rosebank, Johannesburg 2196, South Africa

Registered Offices: Penguin Books Ltd, 80 Strand, London WC2R 0RL, England

First published in the United States of America by Dutton Books,
a member of Penguin Group (USA) Inc., 2008
Published by Speak, an imprint of Penguin Group (USA) Inc., 2010

10 9 8 7 6 5 4 3 2 1

Speak ISBN 978-0-14-241665-5

Designed by Irene Vandervoort
Printed in the United States of America

eeeeee

For Sharle, the best sister an only child ever had

eeeeee

goddess
boot camp

CHAPTER I

HYDROKINESIS

SOURCE: POSEIDON

The ability to control and move liquids. Density of liquid affects level of control. Water is the easiest liquid to manipulate because, with the exception of dramatically dry environments (i.e. Las Vegas, Sahara Desert, Australian Outback), it is always present in the surrounding air.

DYNAMOTHEOS STUDY GUIDE © Stella Petrolas

I.

Am.

A.

Goddess.

An honest-to-goodness goddess.

With superpowers and everything.

Okay, so I'm just a minor, minor, *minor* goddess. Technically, I'm supposed to say *hematheos*, which means godly blood, or *part* god, but goddess sounds much more impressive (to the like ten people I'm allowed to tell). There's no percentage requirement or anything—all that matters is having a god or goddess somewhere up the line, and my great-grandmother, it turns out, is Nike. The goddess; not the shoe. That makes me a tiny leaf on a narrow branch of the massive and ancient family tree of the gods.

So I can say with only minor hesitation that I, Phoebe Castro, am a goddess. The thing is, I only learned this about myself a few months ago—when my mom married a Greek guy and transplanted me halfway around the world to the tiny island of Serfopoula.

I spent the first seventeen years of my life believing I was a perfectly normal girl from a *semi*functional family with a deceased dad and a workaholic mom. Then *wham-o*, I find out Dad's dead because he disobeyed some supernatural edict and got smoted to Hades and I am, in fact, part of the *fully* dysfunctional family of Greek gods. Talk about your issues.

Being part goddess comes with some serious perks, though. Namely *powers*. I can pretty much do whatever I want whenever I want so long as I don't break any of those aforementioned supernatural edicts. These include, but are not limited to: no bringing people back from the dead (not a problem because, even though I'm dying to see my dad again, I don't actually want to *die* to do it. I have a lot to live for—like my fabulous boyfriend, Griffin Blake), no traveling through time in either direction, and no using your powers to succeed in the *nothos*—the normal human—world.

These seem like no big deal, right? Well, they wouldn't be . . . if I could keep my powers under control. But that is way harder than I ever imagined.

My stepdad, Damian Petrolas—part god himself—says it's going to take time and training. Everyone else at the Academy—the ultra-private school for the descendants of Greek gods where he happens to be the headmaster—has known about their powers almost since birth. They started learning how to use them properly before they could walk. But even they sometimes have trouble keeping their powers under control, like last September when my not-yet-boyfriend Griffin accidentally knotted my Nikes together during cross-country tryouts.

Like I said, I've only *known* about these powers for a few months and these things aren't exactly easy to control. Once, I slept through my alarm and tried to zap myself to class before the bell—my first-period teacher, Ms. "Tyrant" Tyrovolas, has a zero-tolerance tardy policy—and wound up crashing a parent-headmaster conference in Damian's office. Can you say detention?

Clearly it's going to take a while to figure this out.

So I could spend more time on my powers training, Damian banned me from running more than five miles a day until school let out (last week, thank Nike!). Even my cross-country coach at the Academy, Coach Lenny, supported the reduced running time. He says I can never race in the Olympics if there's a chance I might accidentally turn my competitors into molasses or something. Only the lure of the Olympics could convince me to cut back on running. That and the fear of accidentally getting myself smoted by the gods. Eternity in the underworld is a pretty big deterrent.

All the time I used to spend on cross-country I had to spend on learning to control my powers. Not that all the extra training helped much. Countless after-school sessions and weekend lessons—with

Damian, Griffin, my friends Nicole Matios and Troy Travatas, various Academy teachers, or, on days when the Fates were feeling vengeful, my evil stepsister, Stella—and I'm still a menace. No matter how many times I close my eyes and concentrate on moving the book across the table, sensing my instructor du jour's thoughts, or manifesting an apple from thin air, it inevitably backfires. Hideously.

Sure, with Griffin's help I figured out how to turn Stella's hair green for Mom and Damian's wedding, but my attempt at zapping myself some new Nikes ended very, very badly. Let's just say I like my toes and I'm thankful every day that I have all ten of them.

Now it's summer break and I still have only limited control.

I'm back to my regular running schedule, training for the Pythian Games trials, which are just two weeks away, and wondering whether my next powers screwup will be the one that lands me in Hades.

Some days I wish I'd never learned the truth. Life would be so much less complicated if Mom had never met Damian. Right now, I'd be back in L.A. with Nola and Cesca, enjoying my last summer before college by spending hours on the beach. Maybe finally learning how to surf from some hottie surfer boy who would totally fall in love with Nola and—

"Phoebe!"

I shudder at the sound of Damian's voice echoing through the house. He sounds really, really, *really* upset.

"Yes?" I answer as sweetly as possible from the relative safety of my bedroom. Not that walls hinder his ability to read minds—or sense fear.

I watch the door nervously. I know it's a bad sign when I see water streaming under the crack, flowing into the grout lines between each tile and pooling in the depressions of the age-worn ceramic surfaces.

"Trust me," Damian says from the other side of my door, "you do not wish to make me open this door myself."

I leap up from my desk chair and, neatly avoiding the rivulets lacing across my floor, pull open the door. "Damian, I'm—"

My mouth drops open and my apology sticks in my throat.

Normally impeccably-dressed-in-a-suit-and-tie Damian is standing there wearing board shorts, Birkenstocks, and a shark's-tooth necklace. Oh, and he's *soaking* wet.

"Omigods, Damian," I blurt, staring instantly at the floor—I do not need to see my stepdad's bare chest, thank you very much. "I'm so sorry. I didn't mean to, um . . ." I wave my hand up and down in his direction, still averting my eyes. "Sorry, sorry, sorry. I was just thinking about how much I miss L.A. and that I've never learned how to surf and now that school's out I could go if I didn't have the Pythian trials and my stupid powers weren't—"

Damian holds up his hand and takes a deep, *deep* breath. He lets it out super slow, with a little bit of a growl from the back of his throat. And then he takes another. And another.

I've really done it this time. I mean, the palm tree in the living room had been bad enough, but he is clearly beyond furious at the moment.

Instinctively I inch back a step . . . right into a growing puddle. The sloshing sound of me smacking into the water breaks his deep breathing.

"I am not angry with you," he says, carefully enunciating each word. "Truly."

I'm not convinced.

He runs a hand through his wet hair, sending a fresh spray of water droplets everywhere.

"Oh, for Hera's sake," he mutters. For a second I'm nearly blinded by a bright glow, and when I open my eyes again, Damian is back to his dry, fully clothed self. The puddles are still there. "Let us speak in my office, shall we?"

I hang my head and follow Damian through the house. Why do these things keep happening to me? I mean, you'd think after all these months I'd have improved a little. At least enough so that things wouldn't go haywire when I'm just randomly thinking about completely non-powers-related stuff.

"Please." Damian gestures at a chair in front of his desk. "Have a seat."

Sinking into the soft leather—hard-core-hippie Nola would have a field day with the cruel and unnecessary use of animal hide—I try to clear my mind of all thoughts. It's thinking that gets me into trouble. If I could go the rest of my life without thinking, then—

"I know you are using your powers neither carelessly nor intentionally," Damian says as he lowers into his chair. "But in the several months since your powers first manifested, your control has not improved. In fact"—he pinches the bridge of his nose like the idea of my uncontrolled powers gives him a headache—"it may have gotten worse."

Worse? My heart sinks. I've been spending hours upon hours working on controlling my powers. All right, some of those hours—okay, *many* of those hours—were spent with Griffin. And maybe we don't *always* spend every second on my training, but hey, a girl can't focus on work *all* the time when in the presence of such a god. Can she?

"I don't blame you, Phoebe. We both know that, since you are the third generation removed from Nike, your powers are stronger than most. It is not surprising that you are having difficulty controlling them." He smiles kindly and my stomach kind of clenches.

I don't need pity . . . I need help.

"I don't know what else to do," I say, trying not to whine. I am so not a whiner. "I'm sorry. I've been working hard. Maybe I just need a little more time."

"Unfortunately," he says, "we have little time left."

Little time left? What is that supposed to mean? No one ever said anything about a time limit. No learn-to-use-your-powers-by-summer-or-else speech. Suddenly I have an image of myself, chained to the wall in the school dungeon—not that they have one, but this is my nightmare and I can be as creative as I want—being tempted by cheesy, yummy *bougatsa* I'm not allowed to eat until I learn to—

"Phoebe," Damian says, interrupting my fantasy of torture and bringing my attention back to his desk—which is, I realize with sad resignation, now covered in the cheesy pastry treat. Damian waves his hand over the *bougatsa*, erasing it as quickly as it came, and says, "Please, try to restrain your rampant imagination. No one is going to torture you for your lack of control."

"Sorry," I say for like the millionth time. I don't mean it any less, but it's starting to feel like the only thing I know how to say.

I shake off the self-pity. Feeling sorry for myself is not going to solve the problem.

Damian leans forward, resting his elbows on his pastry-free desk. "I was hoping this would not be an issue. That you would harness your powers in your own time without intervention from the gods, but—"

"Whoa!" I jump forward to the edge of my seat and wave my hands in front of me. "The gods?"

Damian smiles tightly and tugs at the knot in his tie.

Oh no. In the nine months since Mom and I moved in, I've learned that an uncomfortable Damian is *never* a good sign.

"Since we discovered your heritage, the gods have been closely monitoring your *dynamotheos* progress."

"My dyno-what?"

"*Dynamotheos,*" he repeats. "The official term for the powers derived from the gods. They've been observing you—"

"Observing me?" My teeth clench. "Like how?"

I imagine the sneaky gods spying on me in the shower or the locker room or when I'm "studying" with Griffin.

"Circumspectly, I assure you."

I am *not* assured.

Damian shuffles papers on his desk. "In any event, they are . . . *ah-hem* . . . concerned about your progress."

Not the *ah-hem*. I have a feeling I'm in big trouble.

"The gods have decreed that you must . . . *ah-hem* . . . pass a test of their design before the upcoming summer solstice."

"And what *exactly* does this test entail?" I ask, already fearing the answer. Whenever Damian breaks into *ah-hems* and nervous shuffling, it always spells bad news for me.

My introduction to this nervous Damian was last year when he told me the Greek gods—you know, Zeus, Hermes, Aphrodite . . . those gods—were real, not myth. So there's probably something major—and majorly unpleasant—coming my way.

"I couldn't say, exactly. In my time as headmaster, they have only demanded such a test from one other student." His mouth tightens a little around the edges. "It will be designed with your personal strengths and weaknesses in mind. I can tell you, however, that it will put your powers—and your control of your powers—to the ultimate test. That is why I would like to accelerate your training."

"Why?" I shift nervously in my seat. "When exactly is summer solstice?"

"The precise date is . . . *ah-hem* . . . the twenty-first." He readjusts his tie. Again. "Of June."

"The twenty first of June?" I leap out of my chair and start pacing. "That's only . . ." I count down on my fingers. "Sixteen days away."

"The gods do not prize patience as a great virtue."

"You think?" I ask, pulling out my best sarcasm.

I am not even pacified by the fact that he looks embarrassed.

He *should* be embarrassed. Even if this isn't his fault.

Why does this stuff happen to me? I mean, I barely make it through what should have been my skate-through senior year with a B average. Now, after deciding to stick around an extra year to work on my powers—and to spend another year with the previously mentioned amazing boyfriend, Griffin—I find out I have to pass a test that proves I know how to control my powers *first*. Talk about a contradiction.

"What happens if I fail?" I ask. "Do I have to repeat Level 12, or what?"

"You will not fail," he says, way too eagerly. "You have my word."

"Okay," I agree. "But what if I *do*?"

"If you do?" More paper shuffling. "You will be placed in a kind of . . . remedial program."

There is something more he's not saying, I can tell. I've learned to read him pretty well since he became my stepdad. But, at this point, I'm not prepared to dwell. I have an extreme imagination for coming up with all kinds of crazy punishment scenarios, but in this world—the world of myths and gods and *dynamotheos* powers— sometimes even my worst fears pale in comparison. Prometheus getting his liver pecked out daily by a giant eagle comes to mind. I don't *want* to know what he's not telling me.

"I will not allow you to fail," he says again.

"How exactly are you going to make sure I don't? Do you have some kind of magical get-out-of-Hades-free card?" I pace back and forth in front of his desk. "You and Mom are leaving in the morning for your honeymoon. You can't exactly work with me from Thailand, can you?"

"Of course not," he answers smoothly. "I have already arranged for an alternative training program."

I silently hope this means even more private lessons from Griffin, but I know I'm not that lucky. And Damian's not that considerate of my love life.

"No, not private lessons," he says, proving again that he can read minds. "I have enrolled you in *Dynamotheos* Development Camp. You begin in the morning."

೭೭೭೭೭

"Now I have to pass this mysterious test before summer solstice or I'll get held back a year." I flop back next to Nicole on my bed, staring at the white plaster ceiling while my feet dangle off the edge. "Or locked in the school dungeon or chained to a mountainside—"

"You're being melodramatic," Nicole interrupts. "No one's been chained to a mountain in centuries. And those rumors about the torture devices in the dungeon are completely fabricated."

At my panicked look, she relents. "I'm teasing." She grabs a pillow and smacks me over the stomach. "Lighten up, will ya?"

I try to relax with a deep breath and a heavy sigh. It doesn't work.

Nicole is so much better at the whole go-with-the-flow, leave-your-worries-behind thing. Me? I'm like a poster child for stressing about stuff you can't control.

I don't know what I'd do if she weren't staying on Serfopoula for the summer. Of course, she stays on Serfopoula *every* summer—it's one of the contingencies for allowing her back on the island to attend the Academy after her parents were banished by the gods. She can't leave until she graduates.

That sucks for her, but I'm glad she's here.

"Does Petrolas have a plan to boost your training?"

"Yeah." I sigh, wishing I was a little more spiky-blonde-haired extremist girl, instead of long-brown-ponytailed worry girl. "He's sending me to *Dynamotheos* Development Camp for the next two weeks."

"Goddess Boot Camp?" she gasps. "Seriously?"

Goddess Boot Camp? My stomach knots at the thought of a military-style training program. Multimile marches at dawn. Rope climbs in the rain. Instructors standing on my back while I do a million push-ups. A far cry from the cross-country and wilderness camps I've experienced.

"Is there something wrong with that?"

"No." Nicole starts laughing uncontrollably, practically rolling off my bed. "Nothing"—*laugh, laugh, laugh*—"wrong"—*laugh, laugh, laugh*—"with that."

"What?" I demand, shoving her shoulder so she *does* roll off the bed. "I'm going to be turned into a goat, aren't I? How can I train for the Pythian trials with four legs?"

I follow her off the bed and start pacing.

The Pythian Games are a huge deal. Apparently, the Olympics weren't always the only games in town. When the last ancient Olympics were held in the year 393, the Pythian Games became restricted to *hematheos* competitors and went underground. They've been held every four years—except during World Wars I and II—since forever.

Griffin and I were invited by the coach of the Cycladian team—

who also happens to be Coach Lenny—to try out for this summer's games.

We're supposed to start training today. In fact—I check my watch—he's supposed to be here any second.

"Relax," Nicole says as she pulls herself off the floor. "It's not so much scary as . . ." She smiles. "Embarassing."

"Great. That's just what I need." I flop into the giant squishy chair Mom and Damian bought for my birthday, sinking into the turquoise velvet softness. "Another reason for everyone to make fun of me."

Being the new girl at a school full of descendants of the gods is no cakewalk. You'd think once I found out I was a descendant, too, they would let up. But no. Most of them still treat me like a total outsider. An interloper who can't control her powers. An intruder. Especially after I "stole" Griffin—as if you can steal someone who doesn't want to be stolen—away from cheer queen Adara Spencer. And don't think she has ever let me forget it. When we had to give our final speeches in Oral Communications two weeks ago, she made every word I said come out in pig latin.

Partly, Damian says, it's that I'm closer to Nike than most of them are to their gods. They're jealous, he says. Right. And jerky Justin dumped me because I was too good for him.

"Don't worry," Nicole says, trying to be reassuring after laughing herself into hysterics. "Maybe no one will find out you're in boot camp."

"Really?" I ask, hopeful even if she's just trying to make me feel better.

"Sure." She takes a seat on my bed. "Usually it's just a couple of upper-class counselors, a faculty director, and about a dozen, um, campers."

My racing heart calms down. A little.

"Okay," I say, breathing a sigh of relief. "That should be okay. Maybe the counselors will be friendlies."

Not that there are many. Besides Nicole, our good friend Troy, Griffin, and a couple of my cross-country teammates, there aren't many kids at the Academy I could call friendly, let alone friends.

With my luck, they'll be a couple of Adara's groupies who can't wait to expose my embarrassment to the world. It's not like I can do anything to make them like me since I didn't do anything to make them hate me in the first place. My existence is reason enough for them.

Besides, the truth is I am a little freaked out about controlling my powers, especially considering how my dad died. I haven't worked out all the details yet, but he used his powers to improve his football career . . . and wound up smoted by the gods. I don't think I'll ever know exactly what happened. The gods frown on the misuse of powers in the *nothos* world and they could just as easily smote me for using them accidentally.

Controlling my powers is a good thing, and I'm looking forward to the day when I can zap myself a Gatorade without worrying that I'll wind up wrestling an alligator.

"Who knows?" I say. "Going to Goddess Boot Camp could be fun."

"Goddess Boot Camp?" Griffin asks as he walks into my room.

"Hi!" I jump up and wrap my arms around his neck. Since school let out Wednesday, he's been in Athens with his aunt Lili, picking up an espresso machine for the bakery. I know it's only been four days, but seeing him again—all tall, lean, and dark, curly-haired dreamy—makes me shivery happy all over.

Especially when he's wearing track pants. Call me a running geek, but I love a guy in training gear.

He hugs me back and whispers in my ear, "I missed you, *kardia tis kardias mou.*"

And I love it when he calls me his heart of hearts. Leaning back, I give him a soft kiss. We've been going out for almost nine months, but I still can't get over kissing him. My real-life hero.

"Let me just lace up," I say, releasing him and going for my sneakers under the bed, "and I'll be ready to go."

"Hey, Nic," he says softly.

She gives him a little smile. "Hi, Griff."

"You doing all right?" he asks.

"Always, jockhead."

She means that affectionately. I think.

Besides, all the descendants of Ares are jockheads. But there's more to him. She doesn't know he's a heroic descendant of Hercules, too. No one does.

I take a seat on my bright yellow rug and pull on my Nikes. Even though Griffin and Nicole worked through their major problems last fall—they had been best friends when they were little, until their parents got punished for something the kids did—they're still a little awkward around each other. They both like me, though, and they have some serious history behind them. I have faith.

"What were you saying about Goddess Boot Camp?" Griffin asks as I tie my laces into bows. "Why are you going?"

"Damian's making me." I let out a rough breath. "He's afraid I won't be able to pass the test."

"What test?"

"The one the gods are making her take," Nicole explains.

Griffin scowls, his dark eyebrows scrunching together over his bright blue eyes in an adorably concerned way. "I was afraid something like this would happen. What with your powers still so unpredictable—"

"Hey!" I smack him on the thigh. "It's not for lack of trying."

"I know," he says, reaching down and pulling me to my feet. "It's not your fault. Not with such late-onset powers."

"And the fact that you're only three steps down from Nike," Nicole adds. "They're stronger than most."

I feel a little better. I mean, most of the kids at the Academy are several generations or more removed from their ancestor god. The closer your branch is to the trunk of the tree, the stronger the powers. Mine are colossal strong. Which makes them colossal hard to control.

Clearly, the gods aren't taking that into account.

"Sorry. I didn't mean to snap." Sometimes I open my mouth and my emotions spill out before I can check them. "It's not your fault I'm a complete failure at the whole powers thing."

"You're not a failure," Griffin insists. "Just . . . inexperienced. Like training for the Pythian Games. Even though you already know how to run, you still need to train hard and in a different way for the marathon-length race than you do for cross-country. Right?"

"Of course."

"You just have to keep pushing yourself harder, further, until it becomes as natural as what you're used to."

One of the reasons I adore Griffin so much is his ability to speak my language. Runner-ese.

"What do you think will happen if I fail the test?" I ask. "Damian wasn't exactly forthcoming about the consequences."

Griffin shakes his head. "I don't know. Has anyone else ever taken a test like this?"

"There are rumors," Nicole says. "No one's ever proven them."

"Damian told me there has been one other student tested since he became headmaster. But he didn't tell me who it was or what happened."

Nicole snorts.

We all know Damian's big on secrecy. The man makes the CIA look like a gabfest. He is Mr. Need-to-know. As in, students never need to know.

I close my eyes. It's either that or give in to the despair. Of course I'm one of only two *hematheos* in recent history forced to take a powers test—and likely to fail that test. Life would be too good if I weren't about to be made a horrible outcast. I mean *more* of a horrible outcast. It's bad enough I'm already the girl who didn't know about her powers—and the entire *hematheos* world—until she was seventeen, and the girl who is so close to Nike she makes the other kids nervous and resentful. Now I'll be the girl strung up on the rack for the next seven or so centuries.

Rather than focus on something I don't have control over at the moment—exactly my problem, by the way—I focus on something I can control. Running.

"I can't think about this anymore right now," I announce. I ask Griffin, "Are you ready to run?"

"Of course." He flashes me a brilliant grin.

Turning to Nicole, I offer, "You're welcome to join us."

"No thanks." She climbs off the bed and grabs her messenger bag from the floor. "I'm allergic to exercise."

"So I've noticed," I tease. She and Troy have that in common.

"I was thinking we could run the north shore today," Griffin says. Then to Nicole, "You could walk with us as far as the village." He dips his head a little and lowers his voice. "If you're heading that way."

My fears of smoting and embarrassment and being turned into a goat are instantly gone. I'm so proud of Griffin for making inroads with Nicole. They'll be back to best friends in no time.

"Thanks," she says. "But I'm heading to the library for a little extracurricular research."

Or maybe their friendship will take a little more time to heal back to pre-incident levels. I'm not concerned. They've gone from mortal enemies to friendlies in under a year. It will all be behind them by the time we graduate.

"We can walk with you to the school," I say, snagging an elastic off my dresser and pulling my hair into a ponytail. "Since it's on the way to the village."

As we head through the living room, I hear Damian's voice coming from the master bedroom. "We will be gone for less than two weeks, Valerie," he says. "Is it really necessary to take three suitcases?"

"I've never been to Thailand before," she replies. "I'm not sure what to pack. Besides . . ." Her voice takes on a kind of purring tone. "We only have *one* honeymoon and I want to make it special."

Mom and Damian have been married for months now, but their lovey-dovey talk is still going strong. An image of what exactly my mom is packing in those three suitcases is about to pop into my mind. It has lace and sequins and—I shudder—feathers.

"Let's go," I say, grabbing Griffin and Nicole by the arms and hurrying them out the door. "With any luck, they'll be done packing when I get home."

As Griffin and I round a rocky outcropping on Serfopoula's north-shore beach, I'm thinking about Dad. That's not so unusual. I think about Dad a lot when I run. Lately, though—ever since I found out I was a descendant of the goddess of victory and exactly how Dad died—my thoughts have been a little different.

Before I found out, running usually brought back memories of training with him. Of running on Santa Monica beach in the early-morning hours and getting ice cream when we were done. Of him shouting encouragements: "Feel the victory inside you, Phoebester." (Yeah, *victory* has a completely different meaning now.)

Since finding out, running makes me think about how he died.

About how, even though he knew there would be consequences for using his powers, he loved football so much he was willing to risk it. To risk *us*.

I still can't believe he loved football more than me and Mom.

"How we doing?" Griffin asks, pulling me out of my thoughts.

I shake my head back into the moment.

"That's our halfway mark for today." I point at a low-hanging tamarisk tree at the edge of the beach.

"What's our time?"

Lifting my wrist, I check my watch. It reads 1:42 P.M. Not good.

"Crap." How could I be so stupid? "I forgot to start the stopwatch."

"No problem." He flashes me a quick smile. "We can start logging our pace tomorrow. Today can be a warm-up."

"I don't know what's wrong with me," I say, matching his strides with every step. It's not like me to mess up a training session like this. "Every time I get to the starting line lately, it's like my brain goes to mush."

"You're worried about your powers," he says as we reach the tree and turn to run back the way we came. "Understandable."

"Yeah," I agree, although he's only half right. "I know."

I am worried about my powers . . . but not for the stupid test. Whatever consequences I'll have to face if I fail the test are pudding play compared to smoting. That's irreversible.

"You'll pass," he insists. "Just like you made the cross-country team last year. Just like you got your B average. Just like you master everything you go after with your whole heart."

"This isn't exactly the same." It's not at all the same. "I can't pass this test by running faster or studying harder."

"You'll find a way."

"But what if I—" Aargh, I'm tired of worrying about this. "Forget it. Let's just focus on the running, okay?"

He's silent for a long time and I think he's going to let it go. Which is what I want. Right? Except something inside me is willing him not to forget it. Then he asks, "What's really bothering you, Phoebes?"

"Nothing, I—"

"It's your dad, isn't it?"

My shoulders tense. I haven't really talked about this with anyone since I found out. Not even Mom. She seems just as willing to keep the topic buried as I am. But maybe I need to talk about this. About him.

Finally, after what feels like hours of tension, I say, "Yeah. Kind of."

"Tell me."

As our sneakers push into the pristine sand, I try to form the sentence. Try to figure out how to express what I'm feeling. How can I tell him that I'm terrified every second that I'll cross some invisible line and pay the ultimate price for my mistake? Everything I come up with sounds wrong, childish. Like a scared little girl.

"I—" I want to tell him. Really I do. I want to bare my soul and have him tell me everything will be all right and I won't get smoted to Hades if I screw up. But what if? What if he can't reassure me?

23

What if he can't make a promise he knows he can't keep? I don't think I can face a confirmation of my fears. "I can't."

"That's okay." His voice is soft and quiet, like our footfalls in the sand. "I'm here when you're ready."

And just like that, with one little promise, I feel a million times better. Knowing he's there for me makes the fears fade into the background. Even if it's only for a little while.

Thanks. I don't have to say the words out loud for him to know.

"So," he says, in a cheerful, let's-get-past-this-dark-moment tone. "Tell me more about our training schedule."

I flash him a quick smile, thankful for the distraction. Knowing my luck, the more I worry about the whole smoting thing, the more likely I am to accidentally smote myself.

"It's a tiered program," I explain, launching into the more comfortable topic. "We build up our mental and physical stamina on an accelerated schedule, increasing the workout a little each day. By the time race day is here, 26.2 miles will feel like no big thing."

Because the long-distance race in the Pythian Games is marathon length—and the trials are just two weeks away—we have to train hard and build our endurance quickly. Griffin has never run anything longer than a cross-country race, and even though I've run in marathons before, I've never *raced* a marathon. Running to finish and running to win are two totally different things.

Per Pythian Games rules, Coach Lenny can't actually train us until after the trials, but he helped me develop this training strategy. If we don't make the cut, he's promised to make our lives miserable when cross-country season starts up in the fall.

"Sounds good."

I'm glad Griffin and I are going through this together. Even though I've been running all my life, the idea of actually *racing* those 26.2 miles is a little scary. That's like running a race from downtown L.A. to Malibu. It feels less intimidating knowing he's by my side.

"Wanna stop by the bakery on our way back?" he asks. "Aunt Lili made some *loukoumades* she wants you to try."

"Mmm," I say, my mouth watering at the thought of the decadent little doughnut balls. "I think your aunt is trying to fatten me up."

Griffin's aunt is a descendant of Hestia and, true to her goddess-of-the-hearth heritage, operates an amazing bakery in the village. She makes more varieties of bread every day than most people have ever even heard of. Walking into the store is like walking into a fresh-baked dream.

Lately I've been her favorite taste tester.

"She's just relieved that you eat," he explains. "Adara wouldn't even go near the bakery in case the carbs could seep into her body by osmosis or something."

I fall silent.

Adara is still a dangerous subject. Not only has she not forgiven me for "stealing" her boyfriend—go figure—but Griffin is still friends with her. I'm not jealous or anything, I just don't understand how he can actually like her. She's never been anything but an evil harpy to me.

Griffin, clearly unaware of my mood swing, says, "Aunt Lili is excited that our nutrition plan requires lots of carbs. She thinks that means we'll be in there to taste-test every day."

"Hmm," I grunt noncommittally.

"I didn't have the heart to tell her we need *complex* carbs, like pasta and potatoes." He sounds completely unconcerned by my silence. "Breads, maybe. If she uses whole grains. But sugars and sweets are not exactly ideal training fuel."

When Coach Lenny asked us to try out for the Pythian Games, we agreed to divide up the training prep work. I'm in charge of physical training sessions—running, weight training, stuff like that. Griffin is in charge of our nutritional program. Which is probably a good thing, because I have a major weakness for things like Aunt Lili's treats, the occasional Twinkie shared with Nicole, and—the worst weakness of all—ice cream. I'd eat ice cream at every meal if I could.

It's definitely a good thing Griffin's the diet dictator.

More silence as we both fall into a contented run.

My mind drifts back to the Adara comment. I realize I'm being hypersensitive about the whole ex-girlfriend thing. I mean, I'm *not* jealous. Really. He's totally, one hundred percent into me. And the fact that he's still friends with his on-again-off-again girlfriend of like five years is not completely surprising. They have a history.

That doesn't mean I have to like it.

"You'll pass the test," Griffin says as we get within sight of the village.

I sigh. It's better to let him think I'm stressing about the test than confess that I'm really dwelling on his relationship with his ex.

"I know," I say, trying to sound convincing.

"I mean it," he says, slowing our pace to a light jog. "If anyone can learn to control insanely strong powers in the next two weeks, you can. You can do anything."

I love that he's my strongest supporter, my own personal Phoebe cheerleader. He sounds totally certain that I'll succeed . . . but I'm not.

"Listen," he says, pulling me to a stop as we reach the outer edge of the village. "Think about how much you've accomplished in the last few months. A weaker girl would have collapsed under the pressure of starting over at a new school populated with descendants of the gods. Not you. You thrived and proved to every last one of us that you deserve to be here. And you do."

His blue eyes are practically glowing with sincerity. My own feel a little damp. My only pre-Griffin experience with a boyfriend was jerky Justin Mars—a total sleaze who treated me like dirt and dumped me for an easy squeeze when I wouldn't put out. Having a boyfriend so fully and totally supportive is an experience I'm still getting used to.

"All you have to do is take all the energy you focused on winning that race last fall"—he reaches up and wipes at the tear that escaped down my cheek—"and focus it on controlling your powers. No problem."

I give him a watery smile. I am *so* not a girl who cries. And it's not what he's saying that makes me weepy, but the way he's saying it. Like he believes I'm capable of conquering the world. He believes in me. Unconditionally.

My heart thuds. I've never felt more supported, more confident, more—his eyes glance over my shoulder and focus on something behind me—forgotten?

"Hey, Adara," he says, smiling. "We were just heading for the bakery. Wanna come?"

I turn just in time to see her scoff.

"No. Thanks." Her vapid blue eyes rake over me in an especially-not-if-*she's*-here way. "I'm meeting Stella at the bookstore. We have plans to discuss."

"No problem," Griffin says.

As much as I can't stand Adara, I can't stand the way she just shot Griffin down even more. He's nothing but nice to her and does *not* deserve to be dismissed like that.

Still, I'm going to let it go. She's nothing to me—as inconsequential as air. Except for the occasional run-in like this, I won't have to see her all summer.

But then, as I step around her to pass by, she whispers, "You don't deserve him, *kako*."

Oh. No. She. *Didn't*.

I whip back around.

"Too bad you can't join us," I say, in a totally fake voice. "Want us to save you some *loukoumades*?" I glance pointedly at her hips with a pseudo-sympathetic look. "Better not."

I give her an equally fake smile and then saunter off down the street, taking Griffin by the hand and pulling him with me.

"You didn't have to do that, Phoebe."

"Do what?" I should feel better for putting her in her place—after all, she's the one who dismissed Griff and called me "bad blood." But instead I just feel . . . wrong.

"Be so mean to her." He looks disappointed.

"Why not?" I snap, taking my hand away from his. His disappointment only reinforces the empty feeling in my gut. "She's always mean to me."

"Because it's beneath you, and . . ." His voice takes on that serious, descendant-of-Hercules hero tone. For a second, it seems like he's going to tell me something earth-shattering. Then he says, "You need to look beneath the surface."

That clears everything up. I know exactly what lies beneath Adara's shallow, superficial surface—a shallow, superficial inside. I'm still standing there, confused, as he heads off into the village.

I definitely have the feeling that I just failed some kind of test.

Great, another test I didn't know I was taking.

chapter 2

NEOFACTION

SOURCE: HEPHAESTUS

The ability to create an object out of nothing. Knowledge and understanding of the makeup of desired object is necessary for an accurate manifestation. Attempts to create new or unknown objects may yield surprising and/or dangerous results.

DYNAMOTHEOS STUDY GUIDE © Stella Petrolas

"AUNT LILI SENT THESE for you." I show Mom the bag from the bakery.

Mom is standing at the foot of her bed, staring at the three open—and beyond full—suitcases and ticking things off on her fingers. She looks totally zoned out. She's a bit of an obsessive-compulsive when it comes to packing—which is exactly why I was hoping she'd be done when I got home.

"I don't think I have enough bras," she says, giving one of the suitcases a despairing look.

Since they're going to be gone for under two weeks, I'm guessing she has . . . twelve. And will end up packing fifteen. Just in case.

"One more," she says. As she digs a bra out of her dresser—I turn away because I don't want to see anything lacy or sequin-y or feathery—she adds, "Ten should be just enough."

"I'm impressed," I say, making my way to the head of the bed and carefully avoiding the suitcases as I flop back across the pillows. "I expected you to take a dozen."

She spins quickly toward me. "Do you think I need more?"

"No!" I backpedal. "Of course n—"

"You're right." She heads back to the dresser. "Two more. Just in case."

I could groan in frustration, but: (a) I've been through this whole packing enterprise dozens of times before; (b) I'm too exhausted from the training run; and (c) I'm still dwelling on Griffin. I mean, how can he not see that palling around with his *ex*-girlfriend might be undesirable to his *current* girlfriend?

"What is that?" Mom asks, pointing at the brown paper bag sitting on my stomach. "Do I need to pack it? Where will it go?"

"Relax, Mom," I say, handing her the bag without sitting up. I knew she hadn't heard me. "It's goodies from the bakery. You and Damian can eat them tonight. Or in the morning." I close my eyes and sigh. "Or never."

The bed shifts as Mom sits next to my head.

"What's wrong, Phoebola?"

Her hand smoothes a stray lock of hair across my forehead and behind my ear. Eyes firmly shut, I slowly shake my head. If I talk about it, then therapist Mom might make an appearance. And the last thing I need right now is a shrunken head.

"Nothing." I force a smile as I open my eyes. "Just a hard run today."

"Ooh, your first training session for the trials. How did it go?" Mom asks, proving she really has been paying attention to something other than honeymoon plans. "You're not overworking yourself, are you?"

"We did a beach run," I say, not answering the "Mom" question—like there's such a thing as overworking when it comes to running? "We're increasing gradually, but on an accelerated scale. Don't want to wear out our sneakers." I force a little laugh.

"That reminds me." She gets off the bed and crosses the room. "I almost forgot our running shoes."

While she tries to shove two pairs of Nikes—as if anyone in my family could own anything else—into an overstuffed bag, I go over to her vanity and sit on the little upholstered stool. The table is bigger and older than the one she had in L.A. but it's covered with the same collection of bottles and potions. Pulling the little stand mirror over in front of me, I check out my face. It's not a bad face. My skin is pretty clean and it's got kind of an athletic glow. Decent lashes and—my best feature—nice brown eyes. Puckering my lips, I wonder what I would look like in full face paint. I am not much of a makeup girl, but sometimes I envy those cover-model types. Those Adara types.

I push the mirror away and instead grab one of Mom's perfumes. I love the shapes of all the bottles, but this one is my favorite. The bottle is this long teardrop shape with a gold neck and a crystal ball on top. Dad gave it to her the day before he died.

Pulling off the crystal ball, I spritz a little on my left wrist.

The heavy scent of orchid and plum fills the air around me. Taking a deep inhale, I'm immediately filled with memories of Dad. His smile. His wink. His dirt- and grass-stained football jersey. Him waving to us from the grass-green-perfect turf of Qualcomm Stadium.

It's amazing how a scent memory can make seven years ago feel like yesterday.

As I rub my wrists together, I ask, "Do you still miss him?"

In the vanity mirror I see Mom freeze.

I didn't mean to ask the question. We haven't talked about him since finding out he and I are descendants of Nike. Since finding out he died for football.

I should have kept my mouth shut. Talking about Griffin and Adara would be better than this edgy silence.

"Of course I miss him," Mom finally says. "Every minute of every day."

She walks up behind me and puts her hands on my shoulders.

"Just because he's gone doesn't mean he isn't still with us."

Her voice is so quiet and full of emotion I regret saying anything. She doesn't need me making her cry the day before her honeymoon. And I don't need another reason to cry today.

"I know." I force a bright smile. "Running makes me think of him."

That's one of the reasons I love running so much.

"He's with you all the time." She presses a kiss into the top of my head. "Not just when you run."

Great. More tears. Today has been a roller coaster, and I am so not used to being that girl. I've never felt as emotional as I do right now.

"I just—" My throat tightens, but I make myself say the words that have been churning inside for nine long months. The question I'm afraid to ask, but that just won't stay locked away anymore. "W-why did he do it?"

Her arms squeeze around my shoulders. I cover them with my own and squeeze back. For several long seconds we just hold each other, not moving, not saying a word. Like she's absorbing my pain, and I'm taking hers. We haven't shared such an intense moment since the day he died.

"I can't answer that, baby." Her voice sounds small and quiet and a little lost. "No one can."

Sometimes I forget Mom is going through this, too.

Great, now I feel like a selfish cow on top of everything else. The last thing Mom needs is my emotional mess the night before her honeymoon. She deserves her happiness with Damian.

I straighten up and pat Mom gently, signaling my return to my senses. She gives me one more squeeze before releasing me and turns back to her suitcases. I quickly wipe at the residual tears.

"So, are you all packed?" I ask, spinning on the stool.

She looks nervously at the bed. "I think so."

"Great," I say, hopping to my feet. "Let's zip these up so we can go eat Aunt Lili's *loukoumades*."

As we close up the suitcases I try to keep my mind from drifting back to Dad. Or Griffin. Or anything else that might call back the tear patrol. Between Griffin and Adara and Dad and the powers test, it's a wonder I can go five minutes without breaking down.

"All done," I say, pulling the last zipper tight.

Mom frowns. "Maybe I need another pair of sandals."

"You'll be fine," I promise. "Besides. If you take everything you need, how will you justify buying even more when you get there?"

"I never thought of it that way." Mom looks at me, a huge smile on her face. "When did you get so devious?"

"Well, I *have* been hanging out with a bunch of gods," I say. "Maybe it's rubbing off."

"Come on," she says, giving me a teasing nudge toward the door. "Let's go see if we can sneak some ice cream past Hesper to go with the *loukoumades*."

"Uh-oh," I say, leading the way. "I think you're having delusional fantasies again."

She just laughs and follows me to the kitchen. The day we can sneak *anything* past Hesper is the day Dad knocks on the front door.

∾∾∾∾∾

After being shooed out of the kitchen—not only without ice cream, but also without our *loukoumades*, which Hesper confiscated to serve with dessert (for a housekeeper, she's got skills that would make an army general proud)—Mom and I join Damian in the dining room.

"Phoebe," he says as I take my seat at the ancient table, "here is the information you need for tomorrow."

I take the pale blue paper from him. It looks like one of those back-to-school shopping lists you get from an office-supply store. What am I? In kindergarten? Do I need to be sure to bring crayons and safety scissors?

"What's tomorrow?" Mom asks.

"Goddess Boot Camp," I say absently, reading the introductory note.

Welcome campers!

Dynamotheos Development Camp (colloquially known as Goddess Boot Camp) is a life-changing experience that's also lots of fun. In the next two weeks, you will learn how to harness and control your powers and you will also bond with your fellow hematheos *campers. We hope you will come away with not only a firm grip on your powers, but also firm friendships with the other girls.*

"What is Goddess Boot Camp?" Mom asks.

"*Dynamotheos* Development Camp," Damian explains. "A training intensive for students who have not yet mastered control over their powers."

"And you think Phoebe needs this camp?"

Where has Mom been the last few months? I mean, I know she's been wrapped up in honeymoon planning and the idea of starting a part-time therapy practice in the village, but she can't have missed *all* of my powers-related disasters. Especially not the one that involved her bedroom turning into a Roman bath for a day and a half.

Next on the paper is a supplies checklist.

All campers will need to bring the following items:
comfortable athletic clothing

Not a problem since that's pretty much all I own.

spiral notebook
writing utensil (pen or pencil only, no markers or crayons)
positive attitude

I roll my eyes. *A positive attitude?* What is this, cheer camp? And what's up with the no-crayons thing? Is that really a problem? I don't think I've even seen a crayon since elementary school.

"Her control has not progressed as quickly as I'd hoped," Damian says. "I think she will benefit from the intense training of the camp."

"What do you think, Phoebola?" Mom asks.

I look up, startled. It's been so long since someone actually asked me my opinion on something that affects my own life that I'm not sure how to answer.

"Um . . ." I say, buying time to come up with a response. "I think Damian's right. I'm a danger to society. My lack of control pretty much sucks. Unless you like waking up to a bedroom snowstorm."

That taught me a lesson about wishing for air-conditioning. An island breeze through an open window will do just fine.

"That was certainly a chilly surprise," Mom says. "It wasn't dangerous, though. None of your . . . mishaps have caused lasting harm."

"Not yet," I agree. "But what about the next time? Or the time after that? Or the time after that? If I don't get my powers under control, there's always the chance someone might get hurt."

And I might get smoted for it.

"If you think that's what you need," Mom says, though she still looks worried. "I don't want you to spend the whole summer working. You need to have fun, too."

"I will," I promise. "I can focus on fun and the Pythian Games as soon as I pass the stupid test."

"What test?" She looks at Damian. "What test?"

Jeez, didn't Damian tell Mom *anything* about this? He can explain while I finish reading the flyer.

On the first day of camp we will meet in the Academy courtyard at 10 A.M. Camp will dismiss at 4 P.M. Lunch will be provided. Extra-camp tutorials will be scheduled at counselor discretion for campers needing additional or personalized help. Counselors will wait with campers needing to be picked up on the front steps.

Needing to be picked up? Some of the other campers must be pretty bad off if they can't even go home without an escort. I must not be in as bad shape as I thought.

"The gods are concerned by Phoebe's lack of control," Damian says in his headmaster tone. "They have decided she must pass a test before she can continue her studies."

"What kind of test?" Mom asks.

"I am not certain." Damian clears his throat. "In my only prior experience with such a situation, the gods placed the student in a situation designed to push his restraint to the limit."

"And what happens if she doesn't pass this test?"

I look up when Mom asks this because I want to know the answer, too. Surely he won't be quite as evasive with her.

He doesn't get the chance.

"Evening, everyone," Stella singsongs as she flounces into the room. She drops her giant pink purse—the Pepto color makes me want to retch—on the buffet table and slides into her seat across from me.

"You're late," Damian says, giving her a stern look. He's good at stern looks, a talent I enjoy more when they're directed at Stella than at me.

"Dara and I were going over a few last-minute details for tomorrow." She flashes him her best I-can-do-no-wrong smile. "You wouldn't want us to be unprepared, would you?"

Before he can answer—though I know he would totally say, "Of course not"—Hesper sweeps into the room with a tray full of food.

"Mmm, it smells wonderful," Stella says. "*Psaria plaki?*"

Hesper just hums in agreement as she sets plates down for each of us. Arranged on the oval plate is a colorful bed of chopped vegetables—bright orange carrots, lime-green leeks, and warm yellow potatoes—under a whole fish. And by *whole* fish, I mean the *who-o-ole* fish. Eyes, gills, and tail included.

I suppress a shudder and wonder if moving the carrots and potatoes around on the plate will make it look like I ate the fish. From the skeptical look the fish is giving me, I doubt it.

As Hesper leaves with the empty tray, Damian asks, "I trust you girls will manage all right on your own while we are gone?"

We've been going over this in a dozen different ways ever since they booked the trip back in January. It's not like Stella and I aren't adults. Stella's going to be at Oxford in the fall, and if I hadn't decided to stick around for Level 13, I'd be halfway to USC. I can even vote in the next election by absentee ballot. Not that I can convince Mom and Damian. They seem to think we're still in junior high and totally incapable of surviving sans chaperone without either killing ourselves or each other.

So little trust.

"Of course, Daddy. We'll be fine." Stella looks at me. "I'll keep my eye on Phoebe."

"What is that supposed to mean?" I ask, stabbing at a carrot.

Stella just smiles and shrugs.

I scowl.

This is how our uneasy truce works. She makes obnoxious remarks like that—it's who she is. Queen of the cutting comments. Sometimes I let them slide. Sometimes I'm itching for a fight.

After the day I've had, my tolerance meter is on zero.

Focusing on one of the big fat kalamata olives on her plate, I picture a big ugly beetle. I know I can do this. I'm visualizing the olive turning into the beetle. I can see it. It's going to—

The hair on the back of my neck stands up.

As I stare at the olive, suddenly little black legs that look like licorice laces pop out on each side and start to wiggle around. All right, so the legs aren't even long enough to reach the plate. But still, it's a success. I wanted the olive to become a beetle and it (kinda) did.

My powers control is definitely improving.

At least I didn't conjure up *real* beetles or anything—

"Phoebe!" Damian roars.

I tear my eyes away from my success on Stella's plate.

Crawling up Damian's tie—and along his collar and out of his shirt pocket and over his cuff links—are real, live beetles.

"Good heavens," Mom gasps.

Damian closes his eyes, his jaw clenched in clear loss of patience. Not again. "Here, let me—"

"No," Damian interrupts. "I'll take care of them."

He glows for a second and then the beetles are gone.

Why can't I have that kind of easy control? I mean, I know he's had a lifetime to learn, but just a little taste of containment would be nice.

"Damian, I'm sorry," I say, giving him my best apologetic look. "I shouldn't have tried to use my powers at the dinner table."

"No, you should not have." He releases a heavy sigh. When he opens his eyes, he smiles and picks up his fork. "Let's continue our meal, shall we?"

I glare at Stella, as if this is all her fault.

On the outside, she's all composure and highlights and happy, preppy chic. But her gray eyes are full of smug. Like my reaction—my botched powers usage—is exactly what she wanted. I think she enjoys our not-quite-sisterly sparring sessions as much as I do.

Sometimes I think it's more habit with us than actual dislike. Secretly—and I would never admit this under torture or threats of smoting or promises of ice cream—I actually kind of admire her. She never pretends to be anything but herself. Can't say that about most people.

She grabs an olive—the legs now hanging limp—and says, "I think it's lucky for all of us that you're going to boot camp. Mealtime will be safe again."

She pops the olive in her mouth and I'm only partly satisfied by the disgusted look on her face. The rest of me is still disappointed that my success turned to failure so quickly.

As much as Stella's snarky comment about boot camp bugs me, I know that controlling my powers is really important.

I'm tired of being a supernatural hazard.

After dinner, I retreat to my room and my laptop. I call up my IM chat and am relieved to find Nola and Cesca online. If anyone can cheer me up it's my two best friends.

LostPhoebe: hi girls!

PrincessCesca: Phoebe!

GranolaGrrl: we've been waiting for you forever

LostPhoebe: what's up?

PrincessCesca: we have exciting news

PrincessCesca: I got a summer internship with A La Mode magazine

PrincessCesca: in PARIS!!!

LostPhoebe: omg Paris?!? awesome

PrincessCesca: tell me about it

LostPhoebe: when does it start?

PrincessCesca: the end of the month

LostPhoebe: maybe I can visit you

Paris is only a three-and-a-half hour flight from Athens, and Athens is only a three-hour ferry ride from Serifos—the next island over. I bet once I pass the test I can sneak away for a quick visit. Of course that implies that I *pass* the test and don't end up hanging from some medieval torture device in the dungeon. With all my other distractions, that's nowhere near a sure thing.

For now, though, I'm just excited for Cesca. I know how much she loves Paris *and* fashion. This is perfect for her.

LostPhoebe: that's so awesome C!

PrincessCesca: thanks

PrincessCesca: I'm beyond excited

LostPhoebe: what's your news N?

GranolaGrrl: I might get a summer research grant from Berkeley

LostPhoebe: cool. what are you going to research?

GranolaGrrl: native cycladian flora

LostPhoebe: English please?

GranolaGrrl: the flowers of Serfopoula

LostPhoebe: OMG! does that mean you'd be coming here?

GranolaGrrl: yes!

GranolaGrrl: *if* I get the grant

I haven't seen Nola and Cesca since Mom and Damian's wedding last December. There was talk of me spending part of the summer with Yia Yia Minta in L.A. or maybe visiting Aunt Megan in San Francisco, but when the Pythian Games trials came up, those plans got put on hold. If Griffin and I make the team, then we'll be training all summer for the games in late August. This is a once-every-four-years opportunity, so I can't just toss it aside.

But if Cesca is as close as Paris and Nola comes to Serfopoula itself, then it won't matter if I can't get to Cali.

LostPhoebe: when do you find out?

GranolaGrrl: who knows?

GranolaGrrl: whenever the grant committee comes back from summer hiatus

LostPhoebe: you guys do not know how much you just made my day

GranolaGrrl: something wrong?

LostPhoebe: no, just a tough day

LostPhoebe: so much better now

GranolaGrrl: gotta go

GranolaGrrl: mom calling

PrincessCesca: me too

PrincessCesca: tons of packing to do

LostPhoebe: night girls

LostPhoebe: so glad you're heading my way

When I sign off my computer I feel a million times better. It's amazing what a difference a little chat can make.

As I fall into bed, I'm not even thinking about tomorrow. Or about Griffin and Adara. Or the stupid test. Or Dad. Or accidental smoting. In my mind it's already weeks from now and my two best friends are here.

Now, if only *actual* time would fly that fast.

~~~~~

"Rise and shine, camper."

Through the fog of sleep I hear a disgustingly cheerful voice. *Stella's* disgustingly cheerful voice. I must be having a nightmare. In real life Stella is never cheerful. Condescending? Yes. Obnoxious? Absolutely. Just. Not. Cheerful.

"Come on, Phoebekins," the voice says. "You need to get up and see Dad and Valerie off. And you don't want to be late for camp."

I'm blinded as my comforter is jerked away and my eyes are exposed to the morning sunlight streaming in my window. Squinting, I force one eye open.

"What are you doing in my room?" I grumble.

"Waking you up, silly." She takes me by the wrist and pulls me into a sitting position. "They're leaving in ten minutes."

The instant she releases my wrist I fall back into my fluffy white bed.

But my eyes are open.

As she walks away I eye her warily. It's not like Stella to be so sickeningly enthusiastic. She's more the scowl-of-superiority type. But today, everything about her screams joyfulness. From her sunny yellow twinset to her bright white Keds.

Wait. Stella doesn't wear sneakers. Not even the casual preppy kind.

Something is definitely suspicious.

"Are you up, Phoebola?" Mom asks, poking her head in my door. "You know we're leaving in—"

"I'm up already," I say, flinging my comforter to the side.

"Is Phoebe awake?" Damian asks, walking up next to Mom. When he sees me climbing out of bed, he adds, "Good. Your mother and I are about to depart."

"I know." I rub the sleep out of my eyes as I stumble across the room. "Just give me two minutes in the bathroom."

I squeeze around Mom and Damian and then past Stella, who is waiting in the hall. When did my room become Union Station? Thankfully I sleep in a modest T-shirt and smiley-face boxers.

In the bathroom I quickly splash cold water on my face and run a hairbrush through my hair. I don't have the energy to pull it into a ponytail, so I just leave it hanging over my shoulders. I can always secure it later.

When I open the bathroom door, all three of them are standing there waiting for me.

"For the love of Nike," I say, exasperated. "Would you two bon voyage already so I can go back to waking up in peace?"

Mom gives me a ha-ha-very-funny look. What were they thinking leaving at eight in the morning, anyway? Thailand will still be there in the afternoon.

I shuffle into my room, closing the door before any of them can follow me. Thirty seconds later I've traded my boxers for sweats and have pulled on my All Stars so I can see them off.

In a bizarre little parade, we all traipse down to the dock. Zenos, the yacht captain, is carrying two of Mom's megasuitcases and Damian is carrying the other. I'm struggling with Mom's carry-on—which I suspect has at least a week's worth of clothes. Mom is walking hand in hand with Hesper, who is way more like family than staff. Stella is carrying—yep, you guessed it—nothing. How does she always manage to get out of these things? She's like the Houdini of grunt work. Makes Tom Sawyer look like an amateur slacker.

As Damian and Zenos load the suitcases, Mom faces me and Stella

"Now you're *sure* you girls will be all right?" she asks, *again*.

I'm tempted to employ sarcasm, but the fear that she might actually take it seriously makes me say, "Of course, Mom."

"Really, Valerie," Stella adds. "I have everything under control."

I drop Mom's carry-on on Stella's Keds-clad foot.

"Because we can cancel the trip," Mom says. And I know from the supersad look in her eyes, she'd do it, too. She wouldn't want to— she's been dreaming of this trip for months—but she would.

I scoot the carry-on off of Stella's foot.

"Seriously, we'll be fine," I say, giving her my best I'll-behave-like-an-adult sincerity. "Stella and I can get along for a few days." I don't look at Stella because I don't think I can hold a straight face. "I'll be busy training and going to camp."

"If you're sure . . ." Mom's eyes get all watery.

"Besides, we're on an island protected by the gods," I say, throwing my arms out wide. "What could possibly go wrong?"

I know, I know. Whenever someone says that in movies, something goes terribly wrong. But seriously, this is the island of the gods—they even have the souvenir T-shirts to prove it. There are supernatural safeguards.

"Don't work too hard," she insists, pulling me into a hug.

"I won't."

"Don't spend all your time worrying about the test."

"I won't."

"I wish this was something I could help you with." She sniffs. "I feel so powerless and—"

"I know, Mom." I lean back and give her my best seriously-I'm-an-adult-and-I'm-totally-fine look. "Really. I have to figure it out on my own."

Hopefully with a little help from Goddess Boot Camp.

"The yacht is ready, Valerie," Damian says. "We must depart or we will miss the ferry in Serifos."

Mom's tears start to fall. "I'll call you every day," she says, squeezing me one last time.

"You will not," I insist. "This is your honeymoon. Enjoy it. Don't spend all your time worrying about me."

When she releases me, she quickly wipes away her tears. Stella steps forward and gives her a quick hug.

"I'll take care of your girl, Valerie," she promises.

Okay, I am seriously getting tired of Stella's patronizing comments. Like I'm some kind of little kid who needs to be watched over. She's months—not years—older. But I am not about to try for revenge with Mom and Damian standing right there. If I mess up—or maybe I should say *when* I mess up—they'll cancel their trip in a second. And then I'd feel really, really guilty.

"Go," I say, shooing Mom toward the boat.

With one last little hug, she hurries to join Damian. Zenos unties the yacht from the dock and takes his place at the wheel. As they pull away, Stella and I stand there waving—perfectly fake smiles pasted on both our faces. Hesper steps to the end of the dock, pulls a white handkerchief from her dress, and starts waving it at the retreating yacht.

"Don't worry," I shout as they escape hearing distance. "If I have to kill Stella, I'll bury her body in the rose garden."

Not that we have a rose garden.

I brace myself for Stella to zap me into the water. When she doesn't, I sneak a peek from the corner of my eye. She's still smiling and waving.

There is definitely something wrong with her.

"Are you feeling all right?" I ask nervously.

"Wonderful," she says, never taking her eyes off the yacht.

"Why are you being so—"

"You'd better hurry," she interrupts, turning abruptly to give me a brilliant smile. "Wouldn't want to be late for the first day of camp."

She turns and walks away and I'm left staring after her, totally confused.

"The house will feel so empty," Hesper says sadly, still waving her white hankie.

"If you want," I offer, "I could conjure up a houseguest or two."

"No," she chides with a cluck. "You girls will keep me busy enough. Besides," she says, giving me a sly look, "with your luck the entire Greek navy would appear at our door."

"Hesper," I gasp.

"Run along, girl." She motions me up the path to the house. "Your camp will hold more surprises than you can imagine."

As I climb the path, I think Hesper must be exaggerating. I mean, it's just a summer camp. How surprising can it be?

chapter 3

VISIOMUTATION

SOURCE: APHRODITE

The ability to change the appearance of an object. This results in a lasting, but reversible, physical alteration. Such alterations include changes of color, texture, and shape, but are limited to visible qualities. (See Visiocryption *for temporary changes of appearance.)*

DYNAMOTHEOS STUDY GUIDE © Stella Petrolas

MY FIRST CLUE that something is very, very wrong is the giggling. It hits me like a wave of endorphins as I pull open the door to the Academy courtyard. Girls giggling. Lots of girls giggling. Lots of *young* girls giggling.

When I step into the open, I see them huddled in a little giggling mass around a bench in the far corner. There are at least a dozen of them. And they are all, like, *ten*.

I look desperately around the courtyard for signs of anyone who has successfully survived puberty. No. There is only me and the ten-year-olds.

Sticking close to the wall, I inch farther into the courtyard, hoping there's someone else hiding somewhere. If anything can send a teenager into hiding, it's a swarm of ten-year-old girls. They could repel an invading army, given the right circumstances.

"Then what did he do?" one of the girls squeals.

After a brief hushed whisper another one says, "*Ew!* His tongue? That's gross."

I close my eyes and take a deep breath. Surely there's some kind of mistake. They must be here for some other camp or summer school or something. Maybe I got the location wrong? Or the time?

I twist my backpack off my shoulder and retrieve the flyer from the outside pocket. I'm in the right place. At the right time.

Still, maybe they're here for another reason.

Or maybe I've transported to another universe.

"Hey, are you one of our counselors?" a girl calls out.

They've spotted me hovering against the wall, clutching the flyer to my chest. All of them turn to look at me and then—I press my back tighter against the wall—walk toward me. My adrenaline starts pumping as my body screams for me to run.

Okay, you may be thinking that I have some kind of irrational fear of ten-year-olds. Not true. Fear? Yes. Irrational? Not on your life.

Two summers ago the track coach from USC—my one and only dream college until a few months ago—asked me to be a counselor for their middle-school running camp. It was me and a girl from Orange County against more than a hundred fifth and sixth graders. I still have nightmares.

So when I see a herd of them closing in on me, I kind of panic.

"N-no," I stammer. Then I straighten my back—never let them see your fear. As casually as possible, I ask, "What camp are you here for?"

"Duh," one of the girls says. "Goddess Boot Camp."

My heart drops like a lead weight into my stomach. Nicole's uncontrollable laughter when she found out I was going to this stupid camp now makes total sense.

"If you're not a counselor," another asks, "why are you here?"

"Um . . . ah . . ." I just can't bring myself to say it. "I, uh . . ."

"She's here," a whiny voice says, "for the same reason as you."

I turn toward the voice, hoping my ears are playing a trick on me, but knowing exactly who I'll find standing in the doorway to the courtyard. What have I done to deserve this kind of punishment? Did I piss off the gods in a past life or something?

Seriously, of all the people who might witness my humiliation, Adara is the worst. Partly because I know my hope to keep this under wraps is now a total fantasy. Mainly because I know she will love watching every second of it. From the smug smile on her face, she already is.

She looks like camp counselor Barbie. Even in the shadow of the doorway, her yellow-blonde hair glistens. She's wearing a pair of pink camo cargo pants and a tight white baby tee that says GODDESS BOOT CAMP in glittery pink army letters.

I feel a bit scruffy in my old gray sweats and my I'M THE FAST GIRL YOUR MOTHER WARNED YOU ABOUT tee.

"Welcome to Goddess Boot Camp, Phoebe," she says, bouncing into the courtyard. "We're going to have lots of fun in the next two weeks."

She punctuates her falsely cheerful and heavily sarcastic statement with a lip-glossed smile. For about thirty seconds we have a kind of stare-down—like we're both too afraid or too proud to be the first to look away. The girls around us, sensing some kind of confrontation, start oohing.

"Do you have the welcome packets, Dara?"

Oh no! Just when I thought my life couldn't get worse.

"I can't find them in my bag."

I break eye contact with Adara just in time to see Stella hurrying into the courtyard, digging through her Pepto-pink purse for the missing schedules.

"I have them," Adara says as Stella reaches our little group.

She smiles big as she looks up at me. "Hi, Phoebe. You made it on time."

"What is this crap?" I demand.

"You said a bad word," a ten-year-old says.

"Yes," Adara agrees, nodding at the tattletale. Then she gives me a stern look. "But she won't do it again."

"Can I talk to you for a second?" I snap at Stella, not letting her respond before grabbing her by the elbow and pulling her away from the gaggle. "What in the name of Nike is going on?"

"What do you mean?" she asks innocently.

I scowl. Why is she being so cheery about all of this? "Wait a second," I say. "This is why you've been so giddy, isn't it? You've been plotting all the ways you could torture and humiliate me during camp."

"Don't be silly," she says, still smiling. "Why would I do that?"

"Oh, I don't know," I say. "Because you hate me?"

"Phoebe, I don't—"

"Forget it," I say, fed up. "I'm not sticking around for this. Who cares if I fail the stupid test. I'll just—"

Stella's eyes look over my shoulder and she practically melts. Well, as much as Stella can melt, anyway. Her face gets this totally dreamy look and somehow I know it's not just my humiliation she's been fantasizing about.

"Morning, Xander," she calls out, waving at someone behind me.

I spin around, eager to see who can turn the queen of mean into a total delight. Walking into the courtyard is a tall, brooding rebel boy, dark and dangerous right down to his scuffed motorcycle boots. Without even a second glance I can tell he's trouble. He has that go-ahead-and-try look in his eyes. Like he's always looking for a fight.

He doesn't say anything, just kind of jerks his chin—the way guys do when they think they're too cool to wave—in our direction.

Stella follows him with her eyes as he crosses the courtyard and takes a seat on one of the benches. When he stretches out his legs and kicks one boot over the other, I think I hear her sigh.

Then again, it could have been one of the ten-year-olds, since every last one of them is staring at him like he's the gods' gift to girls. Maybe he is. With his short-cropped, dark blond hair, chiseled cheeks and jaw, and serious set of muscles—displayed clearly in his tight black T-shirt—he looks like he walked straight out of an action movie.

Only Adara and I seem to be unaffected by his beauty. I prefer the dark, curly-haired, distance-runner type. She probably does, too.

"Who is he?" I ask Stella.

"Xander Katara," she replies absently, reverently, still openly staring.

"What's he doing here?" I smile as a thought occurs. Maybe I'm *not* the only grown-up in the camp. He looks like the kind of guy who knows how to wield his powers, but maybe not. "Is he in the camp, too?"

That tears her attention away from him. "Of course not." She looks at me like I just made her eat a lemon. "Xander is a counselor. Besides, the boys' camp doesn't start until July."

"Then why is he here?" I ask. "Shouldn't *Goddess* Boot Camp be girls only?" Like my shame would be any less if there were only girls present to witness my humiliation.

"Daddy made an exception," she says, although she doesn't seem too unhappy about the resulting situation. She scowls at me. "For your sake."

Before I can ask what she means, my watch starts buzzing. I quickly punch off the alarm I set last night.

"Ten o'clock," I explain.

Suddenly, happy, cheerful Stella is back.

"Time to start," she announces. "Let's all form a circle in the middle of the courtyard."

She glances at Xander, who looks completely uninterested in the proceedings of the camp. But when Adara herds the ten-year-olds into position, he deigns to join the group. Stella scoots in next to him.

I hover outside the circle, still not certain whether I'm participating.

"Welcome to Goddess Boot Camp, girls," she says, pulling on her head-goddess-in-charge persona. "My fellow counselors and I are going to make sure this is one of the most memorable experiences of your *young* lives."

When Stella emphasizes the word *young,* I roll my eyes. If she thinks those little digs are going to get to me, she's wrong. Compared to cross-country trash talkers, she's an amateur. Rather than rise to her bait, I just cross my arms and hang back. She can say whatever she wants, but I am not going to lose my cool. I am implacable.

Until Adara says, "Make room in the circle for Phoebe, girls. She needs all the help she can get."

My face feels like it's on fire.

Now, Stella can goad me all she wants. I've learned to ignore her for the most part. But there's just something about Adara—maybe it's my tweak over her friendship with Griffin or her generally superior attitude—that makes me want to fight back. So, when she makes her little snide comment, instead of walking away, I walk into the circle. I take the position directly across from her—which happens to place me between Stella and Xander. I can feel Stella fuming next to me, but I don't care. I'm busy staring Adara down.

"Can we start already?" Xander asks in a bored tone.

"Right," Stella says, snapping out of her minisnit and brightening at the sound of his voice. "We're going to start off with an overview of our schedule for the next two weeks. Dara"—she nods across the circle—"the welcome packets please."

Adara pulls a rainbow stack of stapled papers from her bag and hands half to the girls on either side of her. The girls each take one and pass on the rest.

"These packets contain vital information for camp." Adara holds up a rainbow packet. "Besides the schedule, there are handouts, work sheets, and study guides. The most critical is the *Dynamotheos* Study Guide."

"This guide explains the powers passed down by the twelve Olympians to all *hematheos*. It is the foundation for our training," Stella explains. "We expect you to study it thoroughly. Tonight."

I take the packet Stella hands me and flip through it. This seems a lot like homework—something I was looking forward to *not* doing this summer. As if a work sheet is going to help me control my powers.

"Yes, Larissa?" Adara says.

A blonde girl to my right lowers her raised hand and asks, "Um, if *dynamotheos* comes from the twelve Olympians, why is Hades there? He doesn't live on Olympus."

"No," Stella explains. "But he is one of the six original children of Cronus and Rhea. Demeter gave up her claim to a *dynamotheos,* preferring to pass on her agricultural abilities through outreach and education."

"Oh," Larissa says with a shy smile. "Okay."

"Now let's go over the schedule. And after," Stella continues, "we will do some icebreaker activities so we can all get to know each other a little better."

Even though she can't look at him without being totally obvious, I'm sure Stella means *she* wants to get to know *Xander* best of all. The idea that Stella has a crush and I might get to witness her acting like a lovesick puppy makes me happier than it probably should, but a girl has to take pleasure where she can.

Maybe this won't be the worst two weeks of my life, after all.

ᴄᴇᴇᴇᴇᴏ

"My name is Pandora. I'm a descendant of, well, Pandora. I usually live with my mom in Geneva, but she's doing relief work in the Congo and sent me to stay with my dad on Serfopoula for the summer."

Everyone in the circle says, "Hi, Pandora!"

I swallow a groan. This is like the first morning of every cross-country camp I've ever attended. Only at cross-country camp I at least had hard-core running to look forward to. I don't think I'm lucky enough to hope that after the icebreakers Stella's going to say, "Warm-up's over. Let's run."

We're just over halfway through the circle, with three girls, the counselors, and—joy—me still to give our introductions.

"Welcome, Pandora." Stella smiles sweetly at the frizzy-haired blonde. "What are your expectations for Goddess Boot Camp?"

"Well . . ." Pandora says, chewing on her lip as she thinks. "I'd like to be able to turn my little brother into a toad."

The other girls all laugh.

Stella tsks. "You most certainly will *not* learn that."

"Fine, then." Pandora crosses her arms with a little pout. "Since I live in the *nothos* world, I want to learn how to keep my powers hidden."

"Very good." Stella nods in approval.

Everyone else claps.

I'm secretly relieved, because I need to learn that, too. As much as I love Mom and Damian—most of the time—I don't intend to spend the rest of my life on this tiny island. If I am ever going to return to the *nothos* world, as Pandora put it—a world I happily inhabited until a few months ago—then I have to not only learn how to control my powers, but also how to conceal them.

Xander leans forward and says, "When camp is over, I can help you out with that toad thing."

He seems completely serious—no hint of a smile or anything. That earns him a scowl from Stella, a giggle from Pandora, and an eye roll from Adara. I'm definitely intrigued. This is the most he's said all morning. Up until now it's been nods, raised eyebrows, and—when forced—a grunt of agreement. He's definitely got the whole mysterious thing working.

I never knew Stella went for the jaded rebel-boy type.

"Next," Adara says, moving the introductions along.

"I'm Gillian and my mom teaches here at the Academy. I'm a descendant of Athena, and I—"

"Sorry I'm late."

Everyone turns to look as a woman rushes toward the circle, her sandals smacking on the stone floor with every step. Halfway to the circle, the strap on her tote bag breaks, sending the contents flying everywhere. She drops to her knees, gathering the stray papers back into a pile.

Next to me, Stella huffs.

"Everyone," she says, her voice full of barely disguised exasperation, "this is our faculty sponsor. Miss Orivas."

As Miss Orivas looks up and, still on all fours, waves, Stella points at the papers. They glow for a second and then are suddenly back in the tote bag. Another quick glow repairs the broken strap.

"Thank you," Miss Orivas exclaims, climbing back to her feet. "Don't mind me. The girls are in charge." She points at Stella and Adara. "I'm just here to make sure no one blows up the school."

"Lucky us," Stella mutters under her breath. Then to the group, "Miss Orivas is an academic counselor here at the Academy. She advises *A* through *H* students in Level 13."

"I'm a descendant of Harmonia on my mother's side and Eris on my father's," she says cheerfully. "Which makes me a little conflicted."

Everyone laughs. I force a laugh, too, even though I don't get what's so funny. I mean, I can guess that Harmonia is the goddess of peace and harmony or something, but I can't remember who Eris is.

My total confusion must show, because the girl on the other side of Xander—who seems a couple years older than the rest—leans around him and whispers, "Eris is the goddess of discord."

"Thanks . . . um . . ."

"Tansy," she offers, then leans back into her spot.

Okay, I get it. Miss Orivas descends from war *and* peace. Major conflict.

"My family history made for good conflict-resolution training."

I think she expects us to clap or ask questions or something, but we all look at her kind of confused. Well, except for Xander, who is leaning back on his elbows and looking up at the sky. At the unexpected response, Miss Orivas giggles uncomfortably as she takes a seat in the circle between me and Stella and says, "Please, continue with the introductions."

"Of course," Stella says, but I can tell she's annoyed. Maybe because Miss Orivas separated her from Xander even farther, or maybe because Miss Orivas seems kind of nutty. Or maybe Stella's cheerful veneer is finally wearing off—I knew it couldn't last. In any case, she smiles at Gillian, and says, "Continue."

The rest of the ten-year-olds introduce themselves in that painful, first-day-of-class way. Like you're crazy nervous because you know everyone in the circle is staring at *you*. That was always my least favorite part of back-to-school.

When the last ten-year-old finishes, everyone's eyes turn on me.

I blank.

"Phoebe . . ." Stella leans into the circle and gives me a fake encouraging look. I know it's fake, because she looks totally innocent—and I *know* she's not totally innocent.

"Um, hi," I say, brilliantly. I've never been big on public speaking, even if the public in question is just a small group of ten-year-olds. But if everyone else can do it, so can I. "I'm Phoebe Castro. I just moved here last year. Actually, I just found out about this whole *hematheos* world last year. And then I found out that I'm a descendant of Nike—which totally makes sense, because I'm a runner and I *love* to win. But that's a whole other story."

I know I'm babbling.

I know I'm facing a whole circle of blank stares.

I know I should stop.

"Ever since I found out," I continue, "I've had an awful time controlling my powers. I mean, it's like they have a life of their own. They do things all the time without my even meaning to and now the gods are making me take some stupid test, so I really need to get my act together—"

"Your powers act independent of conscious effort?" Miss Orivas asks.

"Uh-huh." I nod.

"Huh." She sounds surprised. "How does it happen?"

If I knew, I would do something about it. And I wouldn't be sitting in an icebreaker circle with a bunch of ten-year-olds, facing two weeks of torment by my least favorite person on this island, desperately hoping I can learn some measure of control when all I really want to do is train for the Pythian Games.

I must look as sarcastic as I feel, because she adds, "What are the circumstances?"

Oh, that.

"All different circumstances," I explain. "I mean, it happens at home, at school, and in the village. Sometimes it happens when I'm trying to do something, but my mind wanders. Sometimes it happens when I'm just thinking. I don't know why any more than I can figure out how to make it stop."

"Fascinating," Miss Orivas mutters, and starts scribbling on her notepad.

"Most students struggle to manifest their powers," Stella says, as if I need explanation. I do, but I won't tell her that. "You have the opposite problem."

Great, glad I could be a case study or whatever.

"The fact that you are a third generation," Adara chimes in, "means they are stronger than most. You're lucky we only had to evacuate the school once."

My cheeks erupt in flames.

"You're the one?" one of the girls on the opposite side of the circle gasps. I think her name is Tessa or Teresa or something.

"The one what?" I ask nervously, though I know what she's about to say.

She leans forward, stage-whispering across the circle. "The one who *neofactured* lions during the pep rally."

I'm too mortified to respond. No one was ever supposed to know that was me. I was only trying to show school spirit (go, Nemean

Lions!). My mouth just kind of drops open, like if it hangs there long enough something will come out.

All the girls in the circle stare, their eyes glowing with fear and awe.

As if I need another reason for kids at the Academy to think I'm different.

"Okay, then," Adara says, saving me—unintentionally, I'm sure, since she's the one who dropped the bomb—from continued embarrassment, "time for the counselor introductions. I'll go first." She tilts her head to the side and smiles. "My name is Adara, I'm a descendant of Aphrodite, I'm an entering Level 13, and I plan on attending the Sorbonne when I graduate."

Wow. I am totally surprised that she isn't going to Oxford like everyone else. Like *Griffin* is. From what he says, pretty much everyone at the Academy goes there, since the school has an arrangement with the administration. If you're an Academy grad, you're in. No formal application required. That eliminates the background research on the applicants—and on the school.

"Hi, Adara," everyone says obediently.

She looks at Stella. "Your turn."

Stella takes a deep breath. "As I said before," she says, her cheerful voice wavering just a little, "I'm Stella. I'm a descendant of Hera. I graduated from the Academy last weekend—"

Everyone cheers, applauding her success. I roll my eyes. As if Stella's graduation hasn't been the number one topic in the Petrolas household for the last few weeks. By the time she walked across the stage, I was ready to use her mortarboard to put myself out of my misery. I'm so over it.

"Thank you," she says, blushing. "And in the fall I will be matriculating at Oxford, where I intend to study economics."

I zone out while everyone oohs and ahhs. This is a story I know practically by heart. Instead, I imagine what life will be like without Stella in the house. Sure, we've only been housemates for a few months, but it feels like a lifetime. It's like I can't remember a time where she wasn't there to torment me daily. No more desperately rushing to the bathroom, only to find the door locked and the shower running. No more having her knock on my door before sunrise, her face covered in one of her rainbow array of face masks, demanding I return something I haven't borrowed—like I would borrow anything from her prep-trendy closet. No more facing her across the dinner table, worrying that my food will turn into something still living—and knowing I can't return the favor without it going terribly wrong. Life without Stella is going to be amazing. Like a birthday party every day.

Little tingles of happiness sparkle down my arms.

"Great Zeus," Miss Orivas cries.

My eyes snap back into focus. Everyone in the circle is staring, wide-eyed at Stella. If their mouths dropped any farther, they'd be cartoons.

A sense of dread shivers up my spine.

Slowly—in the hopes that maybe if I take my time it won't be as bad as I'm imagining—I turn to face Stella. Nope, it's my worst nightmare. The first morning of boot camp and I've already turned

Stella into a birthday cake. Okay, not an *actual* birthday cake. Just decorated like one.

"I'm so sorry," I blurt.

She has her eyes clenched shut—probably to keep the frosting from dripping into them—and I'm pretty sure her jaw is clenched, too. It's hard to tell under the swirls of blue icing. She is going to smote me faster than I can say—

"How did you do that?" Miss Orivas asks.

I shift nervously. "Um . . . I don't know . . . I—"

"What were you thinking about?"

Yeah, like I'm going to admit what I was thinking at that moment. Stella would not only smote me, she'd make it so torturous that the six-day Marathon des Sables through the Sahara would feel like a stroll on the beach.

"I was thinking about my birthday," I cover. "It was a couple months ago and it was so much fun."

Miss Orivas nods in understanding. Of what exactly, I'm not sure. I know I don't understand.

"Phoebe Diane Castro." Stella's voice, gritted out through tightly clenched teeth, is icy cold and barely contained. If there weren't a dozen people here, she'd probably be screaming like a harpy. She takes a deep breath and then bursts into a bright glow.

I blink into the brightness and then, when I can see again, she's back to her perfect preppy self. There's a tiny blob of blue on her left shoulder, but I'm not about to point that out.

"You," she says, an uncomfortable smile on her face, "will learn how to control your powers in the next two weeks."

I'm ready for a threat—although I'm kinda surprised she'd incriminate herself in front of witnesses—but it never comes.

"You will be my pet project." She eyes me up and down. "If I can't turn you into a proper goddess, no one can."

I'm not sure which thought terrifies me more: the idea that I am about to become the focus of Stella's energy, or that I'm actually counting on her to succeed.

CHAPTER 4

PSYCHOSPECTION

SOURCE: HERA

The ability to read the thoughts and emotions of others. Most hematheos *can only sense general feelings, rather than specific, tangible thoughts. Descendants of Hera have the greatest affinity for this power and can often hear another's thoughts as if spoken aloud.*

DYNAMOTHEOS STUDY GUIDE © Stella Petrolas

GRIFFIN IS WAITING FOR ME on the Academy steps when camp lets out for the second day—which wasn't any more exciting than the first day, unless you count Stella and Adara bickering over whether today's handout was supposed to be green or purple.

"Hi," I say, hurrying over to him and throwing my arms around his neck. "I didn't know you were meeting me here. I thought we were training at six today."

"We are," he replies, hugging me back, but looking totally unhappy.

"Then you just stopped by to see me?" He can be so sweet, especially for a descendant of Ares. Nothing warlike about Griffin. Of course there's the Hercules side of him, too. I lace my fingers through his. "I missed you."

He smiles nervously.

I can't tell what's going on in his head. You would think that after going out for nearly nine months, I'd have a little better insight into what makes his mind tick. But no. *Hematheos* guys aren't any easier to figure out than the regular ones.

Still, I can tell there's *something* he's not saying.

Damian's ability to read minds would sure come in handy right now.

"Actually"—he squeezes my hand—"I'm here to—"

His gaze shifts. His blue eyes look over my shoulder and he smiles.

Before I turn around, I know what I'm going to see.

"Hey, Dara," he says with a little wave.

Adara is standing at the base of the steps, just a few feet away, and looking disgustingly vulnerable. Where is the haughty lift of her brows? The disdainful smirk on her lips?

I frown. This must be her tactic—playing the victim about something so Griffin feels compelled to help her. He swears no one but me and Damian knows he's half descended from Hercules, so I'm sure she's not knowingly exploiting the heroic compulsion. But she's up to something. The stench of *Steal Back My Boyfriend* is overwhelming, even from this distance.

I'm kinda disappointed Griffin would even fall for this.

Turning back to me, he says, "Look, Phoebes, I need to talk to her. I'll catch up with you at six, okay?"

Then, before I can answer—by saying, "Um, excuse me?"—he gives me a quick kiss on the cheek and then jogs over to Adara's side, leaving me in the dust. What is going on here? I feel like a total jealous witch, even though I *know* there is nothing romantic going on between them. I know that. Right? Not on his side, anyway. But Adara . . . ?

Prepared to stake my claim, I start after them.

"Castro!" Stella's authoritative voice calls out, stopping me in my tracks with one foot hovering mid-stalk.

"Yes?" I squeak, twisting around to see her glaring down at me from the top of the steps.

With her fists on her hips and a determined look in her cool gray eyes, she looks like a girl on a mission. And I have a sinking feeling that *I* am the mission.

"You and I need to chat." Clearly sensing I'm about to make some excuse, she adds, "Now."

With a glance at my boyfriend chatting with his ex, I sigh. "Fine."

She stomps down the steps.

"Listen," she snaps. "I've been a Goddess Boot Camp counselor for three years, and I haven't failed a camper yet. I'm not about to start with you."

"So?" I ask, stealing a glance at Griffin and Adara. I nearly pounce when he puts his hand on her shoulder.

"*So?*" Stella repeats. "You pose a somewhat more"—she searches for the word—"challenging educational situation."

"Why is that?" I ask absently.

How can Griffin do that, knowing I'm right here watching them?

The ex-couple move down the path and 'round the corner of the building, disappearing from my sight. I can't believe this.

"Because—and it kills me to say this," Stella says, letting out a severely exasperated sigh, "you have the most natural power of any *hematheos* I have ever known."

Griffin and Adara instantly forgotten, I turn on Stella.

"What?"

I can't have heard her right. That sounded like . . . a compliment.

"Most kids have trouble bringing their powers to the surface. Yours *live* on the surface. They bubble out when you're not even trying."

Is that envy in her voice?

"That's highly unusual. Rare, even. Once you learn to harness them, you'll be at least as powerful as I am." She purses one side of her mouth, like she can't believe what she's about to say. "Maybe more."

"I'm sorry." I shake my head. That *definitely* sounded like a compliment. "What?"

"You heard me," she retorts. "I won't say it again."

"Wow," I say, in utter shock. Stella actually complimented me. I didn't think that was in her vocabulary. I'm surprised she didn't spontaneously combust at the effort.

"Earth to Phoebe," she says, snapping her fingers in front of my face. "Focus on the bigger picture here, please."

I scowl. "How do you know what I'm focusing on?"

She just cocks her eyebrows, as if to say, *How do you think?*

Then it hits me. Her dad has this uncanny ability to read minds—or emotions or whatever he's admitting to at the time. She probably inherited that talent from him.

"What, is reading minds like a Hera thing?"

"Didn't you review the study guide?" She crosses her arms over her chest, daring me to try sarcasm again. "*Psychospection,* the ability to see into the minds of others, is a power derived from the queen of the gods."

"Oh." And I thought I was kidding.

That would be a pretty cool power to have. No more trying to guess what Griffin is thinking or what Adara's motives are. Too bad I'm not a descendant of Hera.

"All *hematheos* have this power," Stella says, answering my thoughts. "To some degree, anyway. It's how the powers thing works. In addition to a primary ability from your specific ancestor god, we have powers derived from all twelve Olympians—which you would know if you had read the study guide. The closer you are on the tree, the stronger *all* the powers."

And I assumed the powers were more of a vague, limitless thing. I never thought about there being different kinds. Or where they came from.

"So I can read minds?"

"Not likely." She snickers. "Only descendants of Hera can *literally* read minds. Most *hematheos* just sense basic emotions or general ideas."

Good. The last thing I need is everyone reading my mind. It's bad enough if Stella can. Especially when I'm thinking about how much she—

"Wait," I say, remembering what caused the whole living-birthday-cake incident. "Does that mean you—"

"Yes."

One word. She didn't even hear the question, but I know she knows.

"I'm sorry," I say, meaning it. I may not like Stella all the time, but she is the closest thing to a sister that I have. Besides, I don't like being mean to anyone—except Adara, of course. It's bad karma or something. And I don't need to invite more bad luck than I already have.

"The bigger picture," she prods. "You can apologize profusely *after* you pass the test."

"Oh, right." I set aside my personal berating. "I'm superpowerful. What does that mean?"

"It means your powers are harder to control. They work with very little effort." She flicks her highlight-heavy hair over her shoulder. "You need to learn how to control them properly so they stop unintentionally going off."

That makes my powers sound like a burglar alarm. Like if I accidentally open the door, I have three seconds to enter the code or the police will report to the scene. At least I don't have sirens blaring every time my powers mess up. Although that would at least let me know when it's happened.

"How exactly do I do that?" I ask. I've been training for months, and they're still out of control. "It's not like I haven't been trying."

"But you haven't had my undivided attention." She smiles smugly. "I can work miracles when I have full focus and a plan."

I shiver at the thought of being Stella's full focus.

"What makes you think you know the magic formula? No one else does."

"Because I've done it before."

"What do you mean?"

"I mean, Daddy told you there was another student who had to pass the gods' test, right?"

I gasp. "That was you?"

"No, of course not." She scowls, like how could I be so stupid? "Under my tutelage, that student passed the test."

Tutelage? That sounds too much like torture.

But it's kind of reassuring to know that other student passed the test. With Stella's help. Plus, that means she can dish some more details on the test. Like what that test will be like and what might happen if I fail the test.

"With this other student," I begin. "How did they—"

"I'm going to go through some of my old training lesson plans this afternoon." She cuts off my question and checks her watch. "Why don't we meet back home at six to discuss the plan?"

"Can't," I say, stifling a growl. She always acts so superior. "Griffin and I have a training run."

Stella turns on her stern face. "I really think this is more important—"

"No." As if *anything* is more important to me than running. "I'll do whatever it takes to learn to control my powers, but I am not giving up running. The Pythian Games trials are less than two weeks away and I plan on qualifying. I can't do that if I don't train every day."

She looks like she wants to argue. Or like she's reading my thoughts.

Read this: *No, no, no, no, no.*

"Fine," she says, exasperated. "How about after dinner? You will be home for dinner, won't you?"

"Sure," I say, even though I wonder how dinner will go when it's just the two of us. We had plenty of dinner-table battles when our respective parents were there to intercede. Who knows what could happen when we're alone. Hesper might have to intervene.

"And if you're late," she says with a wicked smile, "I might reconsider my decision to not seek vengeance for my wedding hair color."

An image flashes in my mind, an image of me with hot-pink streaks in my dark brown hair. At this point, I'm not sure if the image is a result of my overactive imagination or if there's some power that lets her plant it in my mind—I *need* to read that study guide—but either way it's not very appealing.

I give Stella my best glare. "Oh, I'll be there."

ceceee

"Did you have your talk with Adara?" I ask Griffin as we start our run. I swallow my irritation, trying for innocuous. After dwelling on my reaction all afternoon, I finally decide I have to face it head-on.

I can't pretend it never happened, but I will give him a chance to explain.

"Yeah."

That's it. No details.

"Was it something about school?" I probe. No response. "Or summer?"

"No."

We jog in silence for several long seconds. Just when I think he's not going to offer anything more, he says, "It's a personal thing, Phoebes. Adara's going through some stuff and I'm helping her out. There's nothing to it."

"Oh." His sincerity makes me feel like a jerk. "Okay."

I never wanted to be one of those jealous girlfriends, so I'm just going to let this roll off my back like trash talk on the racecourse. That doesn't mean I like it any better than I did two hours ago. But maybe that's my problem, not his.

Besides, I don't doubt his commitment. He can withstand her advances.

This time, the silence is comfortable. We're training on the cross-country course today, a course we've run so many times we could make it blindfolded.

My thoughts drift—like always—to this kind of Zen-like state where my mind disconnects from my body. Not really, of course, but there's a distance that lets me think about whatever—usually Dad—and then link back in to check on my body. It's hard to describe, but it's what gets me through the long races. Only this time, instead of thinking about Dad's smoting and whether he knowingly made that choice, my thoughts jump ahead to my own situation. To my out-of-control super-superpowers, to the test I have no idea how to take, to the camp where I will be spending my days for the next two weeks, the camp full of ten-year-olds, (sometimes) evil stepsisters and archenemies, and enigmatic rebel boys who are supposedly there for my sake—whatever that means.

"What's the deal with Xander Katara?" I ask before I realize I'm going to.

"Katara?" Griffin gets that adorable scowl between his brows. "Why do you want to know about him?"

"He's one of the counselors." I remember him leaning back on his elbows, staring at the sky while everyone else did introductions. "All he said about himself was, 'Xander Katara. Level 13.' Didn't even say who he descends from. Total enigma."

"Sounds like him."

Our arms brush as we squeeze through a narrow section of the cross-country course. Glancing down at where the brief contact left little tingles, I realize I forgot to start the stopwatch . . . again. Quickly clicking it on, I make a mental note to add three minutes to the time from when we started. Where is my head, lately?

No, I know where it is.

"So . . . ?" I prod when Griffin doesn't say more about the mysterious Xander. "Who *is* he descended from?"

Griffin shrugs. "Who knows? He's kind of a loner, like Nic."

She's an enigma, too.

"I still don't know her god." She's avoided the question more times than I can ask, sly girl. "Who is she descended from?"

"If she hasn't told you," he says with a laugh, "then I won't. She just started speaking to me again. I'm not about to piss her off."

"Why the big secret?" Seems like everyone in this world has some whoppers. "What difference does it make who Nicole or Xander is descended from?"

"To some people," he explains, "it makes a huge difference. You know how most descendants stick to their own kind?"

I nod, remembering last year when Nicole and Troy gave me a crash course in the Academy cliques. Aphrodites stick with Aphrodites. Zeuses hang with other Zeuses and, because of the Olympian marriage, Heras. And those are just the populars. Breaking those cliques is practically impossible.

"Well, some associations work opposite," he continues with a heavy tone. "There are some gods and heroes that no one is proud to descend from."

"Is that Nicole's situation?" I ask in a near whipser.

"No, that's just an example." His fists clench, a sign he's processing some serious emotion. "There are thousands of years of history in our world, Phoebes. Not all of it honorable."

We run in silence for a few minutes. I focus on my steps and my breathing, on feeling my core muscles react to the faster pace. Step, step, step, breath. My rhythm. Step, step, step—

"That's weird about Katara, though," Griffin says suddenly.

"What?"

"I wonder why Petrolas made him a counselor?" Griffin shakes his head. "He's not exactly a model student. He got expelled in

Level 10. He's actually a year older than the rest of the Level 13s because he was gone for an entire school year."

Hmm. The mystery-shrouded rebel boy gets even more mysterious. Maybe that's why Stella's attracted to him. He's the complete opposite of her kiss-up preppy-girl style.

"What did he do?"

"Petrolas kept it quiet." Griffin wipes a sheen of sweat off his forehead, then runs his hand through his lush curls. "No one thought he'd ever be back."

I wonder how someone gets expelled from the Academy—where students zap one another (secretly) every day—and then readmitted? Maybe Stella knows what happened. She can be deviously determined when she wants to be. And where Xander is concerned, she is clearly motivated. I don't really get the attraction, though. I mean, he has that rebel-boy image going for him, if you like that kind of thing. Which she clearly does. Me? I prefer the heroic athlete type. I mean, how many girls get to date a descendant of Hercules? One. Literally. Griffin's the only one, and he's all mine.

Of course at first I thought Griff was the bad-boy type, but that turned out to be only one thin layer of his personality. Maybe there's something deeper in Xander, too.

Watching Griff from the corner of my eye, I smile. I don't think I could have dreamed up a more perfect guy.

"Can we run in the morning tomorrow?" he asks.

"Sure," I say, though I'm a little disappointed at the thought of getting up early. It's bad enough I have camp every day on my summer vacation. But better to run early with Griffin than alone at any other time. "Any particular reason?"

"Aunt Lili wants me to go to Serifos with her to stock up on fresh berries."

As we kick up our pace a notch, I try to ignore the sour feeling in my gut. Maybe I just imagined the hint of guilt in his voice.

ecccee

"I found several promising exercises in my files," Stella says as we stack up our dishes and carry them to the kitchen.

I quickly rinse mine off and set them in the near-ancient dish-washer—seriously, it's amazing this thing even has electricity. When it runs, the whole house roars like we're keeping a Cyclops in the basement.

Turning and leaning a hip against the counter as Stella adds her dishes next to mine, I wait for her to say more. She carefully rear-ranges my dishes in the bottom tray. Like the dishwasher cares if the plates are all in the same quadrant.

"I'd like to try the first one tonight," she finally says. "I think it will really help you get in touch with your powers."

Her voice is very calm and reassuring, like an elementary-school teacher's. I'm instantly on alert.

"What exercise is that?" I ask warily.

She closes the dishwasher. "It will be easier if I show you."

Ten minutes later, we've pushed the furniture aside in the living room and we're sitting pretzel style on the floor facing each other.

Though I try to keep my distance, Stella inches closer until our knees are practically touching. She reaches forward and takes my hands, placing them palm up on my knees.

This reminds me of the yoga class Nola once dragged me to. Not really my thing. If Stella starts talking about meditation and asking me to "om" to the goddess Shiva, I'm outta here.

"The exercise is called 'Inner Contact,'" she explains, setting her hands palm up on her knees, too. "The goal is for you to locate the source of power in your body."

Next she'll be spouting Hindi and directing me into the downward-facing dog position.

"Close your eyes," Stella instructs, her voice soft, melodic. "I am going to lead you through your body, and each time I say an area, I want you to focus all your energy on that part of your body. Picture your powers glowing from that spot, illuminating the entire room. Okay?"

I nod. I also roll my eyes. Thankfully Stella can't see, though, since my eyes are closed. I'm willing to give this exercise a chance, but I'm skeptical. All this touchy-feely-New-Agey stuff seems like hooey to me.

"Toes," Stella whispers.

I focus on my toes. Seriously, though, if my powers come from my toes, I think I'd be too embarrassed to ever use them again.

"Ankles."

I shift my focus. I'm not sure how I'll know when I've "found my powers," but I keep trying.

"Calves." She pauses long enough for me to shift focus. "Knees. Thighs."

I follow along.

"Hips. Waist. Chest. Shoulders. Upper arms. Elbows. Forearms. Wrists. Fingers. Neck. Head."

Okay, we've gone from toes to nose and still nothing.

"Now I will move on to the organs," Stella explains. "You will need to shift your focus *inside* your body."

I nod. I'm starting to feel really good. Quiet and at peace. Maybe there is something to meditation after all.

"Stomach."

Nothing.

"Heart."

Nothing.

"Mind."

Noth—

"Oh my gods!" Stella squeals. "That's it, that's it!"

I open my eyes, ready to ask her how she knows, but then I see it. The glow. It's everywhere. It's like my head is a giant lamp and the entire room is glowing in my light. (That sounds gross, but it is breathtaking.)

"Wow, that's amaz—"

Knock, knock.

We both jump at the loud knock on the front door. Instantly, the glow is gone. I lost my focus.

"Who could that be?" Stella asks, climbing to her feet and heading to the door. When she yanks it open, no one's there. The porch is empty.

I join her at the door, confirming that we just got ding-dong-ditched. I bet it was a ten-year-old from boot camp. That's just the sort of juvenile prank they would pull.

"Weird." Stella leans out the door, glancing around, then looks down. "Oh, here's something."

She bends down to pick up an envelope sitting on the welcome mat. Reading the front as she closes the door, she says, "It's for you."

"For me?" I echo. Who would leave me a note on the front porch in such a mysterious way? Actually, who would leave me a note period? Everyone knows I live on e-mail and IM.

But my name is penned neatly on the envelope in a thin, elegant script.

I rip it open and pull out the note inside. My jaw drops.

Want to learn what really happened to your father?
XΣ 597.11 F L 76

"Holy Hades," I gasp. Then my everything goes black.

The next thing I remember is Stella shaking me and screaming, *"For the love of Zeus, Phoebe, stop thinking!"*

Everything in the room is swirling around me—except for Stella, who has me in a total death grip. The living room is a whirl of furniture and plaster. It feels like I woke up in the Gravitron—that carnival ride where the floor drops out from under you as you spin against the outside wall—only it's the room that's spinning, not me.

I blink away all the crazy thoughts of what that note might mean. As my mind shakes off the dizzy sensation, the room slowly returns to normal.

I focus on not throwing up.

"We have *got* to get you under control," she says, smoothing her twinset into place, like we weren't just spinning in a whirlpool vortex in the living room.

Better not tell her what her hair looks like.

"What set you off?" she asks. "What does the note say?"

I'm not sure why I don't tell her the truth. Maybe I'm not comfortable talking about my dad with her, since *her* dad stepped into his place. Maybe I don't want to suffer her inquisition over what the note might mean. Or maybe I'm just so shocked by the suggestion that there might be more to Dad's death than I already know that I want to savor that idea without intrusion. Whatever the reason, I shrug it off with a lie.

"It's just a joke from Nicole," I say, forcing a little laugh. "She's a jokester."

From the way her perfectly tweezed brows drop, I get the feeling she's not buying my story. When her gray eyes glance briefly at the white card clutched in my fist, I *know* she's not buying my story. Darn *psychospection*. But, for whatever reason, she doesn't call me out. I can see the instant she decides not to argue; she looks back into my eyes and exhales.

"Whatever," she says dismissively. "Now that we know your powers come from the mind, I can tailor some camp exercises to meet your needs."

Before she clomps out of the room, she tosses another look at the note. A little reminder that she knows I lied.

"Oh, and Phoebe?" she calls out over her shoulder as she disappears into the hall. "Try to control your thoughts until we get you straightened out."

That's going to be a problem. Now that the seeds of doubt are planted, how am I ever going to stop thinking about Dad, and what I *don't* know about his untimely smoting? And worrying whether I'm destined for a smoting of my own?

chapter 5

AEROKINESIS

SOURCE: ARTEMIS

The ability to control and move air and wind. This can also result in the moving and/or levitating of objects, self, or others. Useful during summer months to reduce air-conditioning costs. Only very powerful hematheos can use this power to effect noticeable changes in weather.

DYNAMOTHEOS STUDY GUIDE © Stella Petrolas

"WHAT ELSE DID THE NOTE SAY?" Nicole asks.

After the early-morning training run with Griffin, I'd showered and gotten changed for camp with more than an hour to spare. Since Griffin was on the boat to Serifos with Aunt Lili, I headed to Nicole's dorm room.

"Here," I say, pulling it out of the back pocket of my jeans. I tried to leave it on my desk when I left home, but couldn't walk away. Like I was compelled to take it with me. "You can read it."

Nicole looks at the note and then scowls. "This is the note?"

"Yeah." I lean over and read it upside down. "That's it."

She looks at me like I'm crazy. "It's blank."

"No it's not," I argue. I point at the words. "Right there it says, 'Want to learn what really happened to your father?'"

Nicole squints at it. Holds it up to her nose. Flips it over and looks at the back. She shakes her head.

"Seriously," she says, giving it one last look. "I don't see anything."

How is that possible?

"It must be cursed," she says, handing it back to me.

"Cursed?" I squeak, dropping the note like she'd said it was coated in the plague. I do *not* like the sound of that.

"Relax." She drops back onto her bed, grabbing a black pillow and tossing it in the air. "A curse isn't necessarily a bad thing. It's just a specialized use of powers that affects only one person or a specific group of people."

Snatching the note back off the floor, I say, "Oh, well, that's a—"

"Of course it *can* be a bad thing," she adds, ruining my moment of relief. She snorts. "A *really* bad thing."

"Not helping." I sit in her desk chair and read the note aloud again.

"What was that last bit?" she asks.

"X Sigma 597.11 FL76." It makes no sense. It's not even a word. "What is it? Some kind of code or something?"

"It seems familiar," she says.

Nicole jumps up and grabs a scrap of paper and a pencil with a skull-and-crossbones eraser at the end. Handing them to me, she says, "Write it out. Exactly as it is in the note."

When I do, she claps her hands. "I know what that is!"

"You do?"

"Yes." She smiles triumphantly. "It's a call number. Like from the library."

A call number? I shake my head.

"It's a book!"

"Oh," I say brilliantly. A book. How is some book supposed to explain something about my dad? It's not like just anyone can publish stuff about the secret world of the gods. Mount Olympus totally has supernatural protections against that kind of thing. Why would this crazy note have a library call num—

"What are you waiting for?" Nicole demands, grabbing me by the wrist and pulling me to the door. "Let's go to the library."

I've never seen Nicole get so excited about anything—except that time she came up with the plan to help me capture and then break Griffin's heart. That time didn't turn out so well for me. She temporarily zapped away my ankle muscles so Griff would have to carry me home. That was before they made up, of course. And before he and I got together.

It was the thrill of strategy and espionage that excited her then. It's a good bet that it's the same thrill that has her hurrying me across the campus lawn. In under two minutes we've made it from her room to the library door.

I'd been to the library dozens of times during the school year. Researching a book-length term paper for Ms. T's lit class. Using the computer lab to check out a supercool 3-D physics simulator program in Ms. Madrianos' class. Looking up newspaper accounts of my dad's death.

Still, as Nicole and I walk through the glass double doors, I can't help staring in awe.

You know what most high-school libraries are like? Small, cramped, and with so few books that if every student checked one out at once, the shelves would be empty? Well the Academy library is *so* not like that.

First of all, it's *huge*. When you walk in, you're on the second story, on a balcony that overlooks the basement-level main floor. Circling the upper level is an alternating pattern of tables and chairs, individual study carrels, and comfy armchairs facing low coffee tables. Who wouldn't want to study in here?

Second of all, it's *beautiful*. There is light everywhere on the balcony and pouring into the open space below. Since it's at the corner of the school, it has two full walls of windows that let in glorious sun all day. The shelves that line the balcony are the exact same color as the Academy exterior, so they blend right in with the walls. Everything is trimmed in gold—I have a feeling it's *real* gold—and marble. All the fabrics are this gorgeous gold swirly-girly pattern. As far as lush interiors go, it could rival any of the great palaces of the world.

Third of all, it's *full of books*. Oh, not so much that you feel crowded by them or anything, but if they had a card catalog—which they haven't since computerizing everything in the nineties—it would be the size of an average high-school library. Almost all of the books are in the basement level, which spreads out under the entire school. Probably farther. This is totally the kind of place that would have secret chambers or hidden passages or something else right out of a Nancy Drew novel.

"Come on," Nicole calls out as she heads for the sweeping stair-case that leads to the lower level. "Let's check the call number against the Map."

Note clutched in my hand, I hurry after her. The Map is a huge-scale, Plexiglas floor plan of the library that details what's on every shelf. Not to the book, of course—wouldn't that be cool, though, if it was some ultrahip, interactive map where you could scan through every book on the shelf!—but by call number.

When we reach the map I unfold the note and read the call number out.

"X Sigma 597.11 FL76." I'm sure that makes sense to *somebody*—librarians, probably—but to me it's just a garble of numbers and letters.

The one bad thing about the Academy library is that nothing is in order. At least, not call-number order. Or any other order, as far as I can see. Tracing over the Map with our fingers, Nicole and I search every inch of it. I'm just about to give up, when she says, "Here it is." Followed immediately by, "No, that's not it."

"What?" I move to her side of the Map and look at the spot she's pinpointing with her finger.

"This doesn't make any sense," she says. "That set of shelves has all the X-whatevers *except* X Sigma. There's no X Sigma anything anywhere."

Leaning in for a closer view, I see she's right. How weird is that? The label lists everything that starts with *X* plus a letter from the Latin alphabet.

I scan the Map again. There are *no* call numbers with Greek letters. But the second letter of the call number is definitely a Σ. A Sigma.

Maybe the note was a typo.

"You will not find Chi Sigma on the Map."

Nicole and I both spin around. I don't know about Nicole, but my heart is racing. I feel like we got caught sneaking into school after dark, not searching for a library book.

Standing right behind us is the librarian, Mrs. Philipoulos. I adore her—she helped me find obscure Aristotle writings for my final in Mr. Dorcas's philosophy class—but she scares me a little. She is no stereotypical librarian. She only comes up to my chin, making her maybe five foot. Maybe. My best guess at her age is seventy, but you wouldn't know it from how she's dressed. It's not every day you see a five-foot, seventy-year-old librarian wearing black cargo pants and a black leather corset top. And certainly not one that looks *good* in that outfit.

"Mrs. Philipoulos," Nicole gasps. "You scared the Hades out of us."

"We librarians have to be stealthy." She shrugs her tiny shoulders. "How else can we expect to spy on young lovers in the stacks?"

My cheeks flush with the memory of one night during finals week when Griffin and I slipped down the modern-dramatic-theory aisle for a make-out session, certain that no one in their right mind would come looking for one of those books. We quadruple-checked that no one was around. There was no way she could have—

"Mrs. Philipoulos!" I gasp.

The tiny librarian winks at me.

I give her a weak smile.

Remembering why we're here—and desperate to deflect my embarrassment—I ask, "Why won't we find Chi Sigma on the Map?"

Why didn't we guess that the *X* was really a chi?

"Because," she says, her ruby-glossed lips smiling mischievously, "that is one of the secret collections."

"Secret collections?" I repeat. Why would someone send me a call number for a book in a secret collection?

"One of?" Nicole gasps. "You mean there's more than one?"

"Of course, dear." Mrs. Philipoulos turns sharply and walks to her desk.

"She's a little scary," I whisper.

Nicole whispers back, "She's a descendant of Nemesis."

Who is that? I shake my head.

"Goddess of retribution," Nicole explains.

I'm impressed. "No wonder she looks like she can kick butt."

"She also has excellent hearing," Mrs. Philipoulos says as we reach her desk. Before we can react, she says, "What is the exact call number, dear?"

As I read it out she quickly keys in the letters and numbers.

"Interesting," Mrs. Philipoulos says, squinting at the screen. Her short, spiky gray hair glows blue in the light from her flat-panel monitor.

"What?" Nicole and I both ask, hurrying around the desk to see.

Mrs. Philipoulos presses a red button on her keyboard and the screen goes blank just as we catch a glimpse.

"I'm sorry, girls," she explains, "but that segment of the collection is off-limits to students."

"What do you mean?" I ask. "Isn't this a student library?"

"Of course." She gives me a sad look. "But we are also the official archival library of Mount Olympus."

"So?" Nicole asks, defiantly crossing her arms over her chest.

"So," Mrs. Philipoulos replies, just as defiantly, "not every document the gods file is fit for student eyes."

My shoulders slump. After all the racing my brain has done since I got that note, I half expected some kind of miracle in that call number. I'm not sure what kind of miracle, but I was sure there was some kind of mystery about my dad's death that might explain why he'd died. Why he'd done it. Why he'd decided that his football career was the most important thing in his life. Some clue to how I might avoid the same fate.

Now I might never know.

"That's all right, Mrs. Philipoulos," I say, defeated. "Thanks for your help."

Nicole gapes at me. "What?" she asks. "You're giving up? When you're this close"—she holds up her palms half an inch apart—"to finding the truth?"

"What truth?" I throw back. "My dad died. The gods smoted him because he abused his powers to succeed in football. Nothing can change that."

"How can you be—"

Mrs. Philipoulos gasps, stopping Nicole midsentence. "You're Nicky Castro's daughter."

"Did you know my dad?"

"No, not personally." She gives me a sad, sympathetic smile. "But I knew of him." After a thick beat, she adds, "Everyone did."

My eyes water. There's something in that beat, in that silence, that tells me the entire *hematheos* world knows Dad's story. Like he's a warning. Careful how you use your powers or this will happen to you.

"How did you get this call number?" she asks. "It's not student-accessible in ECHO."

I shrug as I blink away the moisture. "Someone left that note at my door."

"I always say there are exceptions to every rule, honey." She types another quick sequence, turns the monitor to face me, and says, "You have every right to see this."

Nicole hurries around to look over my shoulder as I quickly scan the entry on the screen.

Collection: Mt. Olympus Archives
Title: Council Court Minutes
Topic: Proceedings of the Trial of Nicholas Andrew Castro
Copies: 1
Call Number: XΣ 597.11 FL76
Location: B2-S18D

My heart thuds into my throat.

The record of my dad's trial? I didn't even know there had *been* a trial. I thought the gods just decided among themselves to punish him. If there was a trial, maybe there was testimony or interviews or some kind of documentation to prove that Dad hadn't just sacrificed everything for a sport.

"Follow me, girls," Mrs. Philipoulos says, grabbing a set of keys from her desk drawer.

"I can't believe it," I say to Nicole as we follow Mrs. Philipoulos through the doorway that leads to the stacks. "The record of my dad's trial. I didn't know they kept that sort of record."

I'd heard about the "secret" collection—everyone has. But I had no idea what they held.

"Neither did I." Nicole's voice sounds strange.

When I look, she's staring straight ahead, her eyes completely blank. Without question I know what she's thinking about: the trial where her and Griffin's parents got banished. The trial over something she and Griffin did, and for which their parents were punished. Though she and Griff are finally friends again after years of hating each other over it, I know it still kills them inside. I can see it sometimes when Griffin runs. His bright blue eyes get a faraway look and I know he's thinking about his parents. My heart breaks every time.

As we reach the end of one row of stacks, Mrs. Philipoulos stops in front of a janitor's closet and whips around to face us.

"What I am going to show you," she says, sounding very ominous, "you are not to breathe a word about to another living soul." She starts to turn around and then spins back. "Or a dead one."

Nicole and I exchange raised eyebrows.

Mrs. Philipoulos unlocks the janitor's closet and walks inside.

When we don't follow, she leans her head back out and says, "What are you waiting for?" She waves us inside. "This way."

Nicole raises her finger to her temple and makes the universal sign for nutso. But really, what have we got to lose?

I shrug and take a step into the closet. As soon as we're both inside, Mrs. Philipoulos pulls the door shut. While we're surrounded by darkness I hear a bit of a shuffle. Something falls over, crashing to the floor.

"Drat!" Mrs. Philipoulos snaps. "Who put that mop there? Ah, here we go."

I hear a soft click. All at once the tiny closet is bathed in soft light. And it starts to move. Down.

"Whoa," Nicole gasps. "There's a *sub*-sublevel?"

Mrs. Philipoulos winks at her.

Seconds later, the closet stops moving and Mrs. Philipoulos reaches for the handle. "Remember, girls," she says, turning the handle. "You were never here."

"Oh. My. *Gods*."

I can't believe what I'm seeing. It's a whole other level that spreads out beneath the school. With just as many rows and rows of bookshelves as the floor above. And every last shelf is full.

"Are these *all* records from Mount Olympus?" Nicole asks, gaping just as seriously as I am.

"Of course not," Mrs. Philipoulos says, as if *that's* the most ridiculous thing that's been said all day. "Most of these are from the Library of Alexandria."

"The Library of Alexandria?" I ask. "Didn't that burn down?"

Mrs. Philipoulos scoffs. "Damn fool Hypatia. Athena tried to convince her to install a sprinkler system. But *no-o-o,* no one was going to tell the librarinatrix how to run *her* library." As she starts stomping down one aisle, she adds, "Athena saved the collection before it turned to ash, but she couldn't exactly advertise the fact, could she? So, we keep it protected here."

As we hurry past shelf after shelf of ancient books and scrolls and papers, bound in various earthy shades of leather and smelling like dirt and mold and century upon century of history, I try to catch a few titles. *The Complete Plays of Sophocles. Plato's Early Writings. Chronicle of the Trojan War.* Wow.

Behind me, Nicole gasps. I notice her stop and stare at a book. She runs her fingertips reverently over the burgundy leather spine before tugging it out. Mrs. Philipoulos doesn't notice, but I have a feeling she would freak out a little if she saw Nicole grabbing something off the shelf. I try to distract her.

"How do you keep track of it all?" I ask.

"Hephaestus designed an amazing computer system that scans, categorizes, and keeps track of every document." She keeps hurrying down the aisle, getting farther and farther from Nicole. "He's not just the god of blacksmithing, you know."

"Yeah," I say, picturing his computer-geeky descendants. "I know."

"Aha!" she explains, pulling to stop. "Here we go. Shelf B2-S18D."

She quickly skims a finger across a shelf of books, mumbling the call numbers as she goes. "Chi Sigma 597.10, Chi Sigma 597.1099, Chi Sigma 597.121—wait a second," she says, skimming back a few books and then ahead again. "Chi Sigma 597.1099 and then Chi Sigma 597.121. Where is Chi Sigma 597.11?"

I look for myself. She's right. The book is gone.

"That's not possible," she says. "This is a noncirculating collection. No one can check out an Olympic record. No one."

My heart sinks.

Great. The one and only record of my dad's trial is missing. That's like waving a bowl of cookies and cream under my nose and then telling me ice cream's off-limits. Almost having that record in my hands makes me even more desperate to know everything. All of a sudden I have a million more questions. What's in the record? Who took it? Why did they take it? And, most important at the moment, does whoever sent me that note know where it is?

ഇഇഇഇഇ

"Afraid I won't catch you?"

I look back over my shoulder at Xander, standing there looking all cool and passive. He's holding his hands out, palms up, but in a casual way.

"You're not exactly inspiring confidence," I say, nodding at his hands. "Besides, I've done this same thing like a million times before. It's stupid."

All around me, ten-year-olds are giggling. We're in the courtyard again, though I think we should really be on a softer surface. At the moment we're supposed to be doing that team-building trust exercise where you fall back and someone catches you. I'd much rather crash on grass than on the hard-tile mosaic of the courtyard floor.

All the giggly girls have been paired up, and one after another, they're falling back into one another's arms.

"You almost let me fall!" one girl—Larissa, I think—squeals. She's a descendant of Hades, but with her golden blonde hair and dark green eyes, she doesn't look like any Hades descendant I've met.

"I did not!" her partner, curly-haired Gillian, protests. "I was just softening your fall."

While they argue, I turn my attention back to Xander, who is still watching me patiently.

"You're right," I say. "I don't trust you."

He shrugs. "This exercise isn't about trusting me."

I scowl. "It's not?"

"No." He shakes his head slowly. "It's about trusting yourself."

"I don't get it."

He just shrugs again and holds out his hands.

Clearly, explanation time is over.

I debate it for a minute longer. I mean, he's definitely strong enough to catch me—that's why I'm paired with him and not a ten-year-old—and definitely more likely than Stella or Adara to catch me. But the question is: *Will* he catch me? There's a dark spark of mischief in his lavender eyes that suggests he likes breaking rules no matter the consequences. He's trouble and likes it that way.

"Tell me something about yourself first." I'm not about to risk bodily injury trusting someone who won't tell me more than his name and grade.

He looks indifferent. "Like what?"

"Like—" I almost ask why he got expelled, but then change my mind. That might be too personal for a first question. And after what Griffin said about some people being touchy about their ancestor god, that's not a smart choice, either. Instead, I go for something safe . . . ish. "Are you subjecting yourself to weeks of ten-year-olds just to spend time with Stella?"

I am totally bluffing. I mean, he's shown no indication so far that he's interested in *anything* about this camp, let alone one of the counselors. But she's definitely interested in him. I'm looking out for my girl, testing the waters to see if her crush might be reciprocated. Maybe plant the seed of interest in his mind.

I don't expect an admission.

His dark blond brows lift just the tiniest bit, betraying his surprise. Then, shocking the crap out of me, a flush of pink crawls up his neck.

Gotcha!

He grumbles, "Let's just get on with the exercise."

"Fine," I say, satisfied with my victory.

Besides, if he drops me, I'll have an excuse to skip out on the rest of these stupid exercises. I'll be bleeding from the head, but I'll be doing it at home.

Holding my arms straight out to the side, I close my eyes and fall.

Halfway to the ground, my eyes fly open. He's not going to catch me. He's not going to—

A split second before I hit the ground, his hands slip under my pits. My heart racing, I scramble upright and whirl around. "You almost let me drop!"

"You did not trust."

"Of course not!" I smack him on the shoulder. Hard. "You were going to let me fall."

"No."

"No?" My jaw drops. "My skull was inches from tile."

"Did it *hit* the ground?"

"Well, no," I stammer. "But if you had—"

"Everything all right here?" Stella chirps. She's been making her rounds of the partners, checking on the whole I-trust-you-you-trust-me status.

"No," I snap. "It's not all right. He sucks as a partner."

Stella glares at me. Right, like she'll listen to any words against Xander.

"This exercise," she says slowly, "is not about your partner."

I just cross my arms. As if anything I say is going to convince her that Xander's at fault here.

"Hold this for me." She hands Xander—who spears me with a nervous scowl—her clipboard. Holding out her hands, she says, "Try with me, Phoebe."

"Yeah, right."

Her jaw clenches so tight I can see it.

"Just try," she practically growls.

Fine. Whatever. I spin around, fling out my arms, and hesitate. My heart is still pounding from my almost crash with Xander.

"This time," Stella says, her voice soft and reassuring, "don't think about trusting me to catch you."

"Good," I retort. "Because I don't."

"Instead," she continues like I didn't snap at her, "think about trusting yourself not to fall."

"What?" That doesn't even make any sense.

"Just try it."

Fine, closing my eyes and taking a deep breath, I think, *I. Will. Not. Fall.*

I fall back.

She catches me yards before I hit the ground.

I hear clapping.

When I open my eyes, I see Stella and Xander on either side of me, standing over me.

"Congratulations," Stella says, beaming. "You just earned your first merit badge."

I stare at her clapping hands. "You're not holding me," I say stupidly.

She shakes her head.

"Then who—"

I twist my head back. No one is there.

"You are," Stella says triumphantly.

I crash to the ground in a heap.

CҺAPTЄR 6

PSYCHODICTATION

SOURCE: ATHENA

The ability to communicate telepathically, whether in words, feelings, or other ways, with another hematheos. *Communication should not be attempted without proper training, because of rare but serious risk of brain aneurism.* (See *Psychospection* for the ability to read another's thoughts.)

DYNAMOTHEOS STUDY GUIDE © Stella Petrolas

WHEN I PUSH THROUGH the glass door of the ice-cream parlor, the owner waves. "Afternoon, Phoebe."

I tell myself Demetrius knows my name because he prides himself on knowing *every* student's name—not because I have an ice-cream problem or anything.

"How was camp today?" he asks.

Demetrius, a descendant of Clio—the muse of history—and a major throwback to the fifties, keeps the place in perfect *Happy Days* style. Chrome and sky-blue vinyl everywhere. A long bar with round, counter-height stools. A pair of cramped booths in the back with mini-jukeboxes on the tables. And just about any ice-cream flavor you could ever imagine.

I shrug. "Fine."

"Phoebe," Nicole calls out from one of the booths.

Troy waves and says, "Hey!"

"Be right there," I say, then turn to Demetrius to place my order. "I'll have my usual."

My mouth starts salivating at the thought of that perfectly spherical scoop of mint chocolate chip perched on a crunchy brown sugar cone. Knowing Griffin is going to crack down on our training nutritional plan any minute now makes the indulgence even more enticing. Allure of the forbidden and all that.

"Not today," Demetrius says. "I've got something better."

Better? What could be better?

"Try this," he says. "On the house."

I take the cone and eye it suspiciously. It looks like pretty average ice cream—vanilla colored with little white flecks.

"Thanks," I say, a little defeated. But it's not like I can resent free ice cream.

"Try it."

With a shrug, I dart out my tongue for a quick sample. My taste buds explode with a long-forgotten flavor.

"Oh my gods," I gasp, staring at Demetrius. "You didn't!"

He smiles smugly. "I did."

Nicole, tired of waiting for me, shouts out, "He did what?"

I stare, wide-eyed, at my new favorite person on the planet.

"This ice-cream genius," I say between licks, "re-created Ben & Jerry's White Russian. Perfectly." I shake my head in awe. "My all-time favorite."

Demetrius winks at me. "You're welcome."

"I could just jump over this counter and hug you." I take another lick.

He actually blushes. "Go on," he says, gesturing me away. "Your friends are waiting."

"Thanks."

As I slide into the sky-blue booth next to Nicole, Troy asks, "Why are you getting apoplectic over ice cream?"

"This isn't just any ice cream," I explain. "This is the best flavor ever invented. B&J discontinued it years ago and I haven't had a taste since. Here," I say, holding out the cone, "try it."

Troy turns kind of green and shakes his head adamantly.

"What's wrong?" I ask, jabbing the ice cream in his direction.

"Oh gods," Troy yelps, then claps one hand over his mouth and the other over my wrist, shoving me away.

"What's wrong with him?" I ask Nicole.

"When he was in Athens last week," she says, giving Troy a sympathetic look, "he finally told his parents he wants to be a musician."

"Good for you!" I congratulate Troy, who still looks more green than not. We've been trying to get him to come clean for months. He's from a long line of doctors—like millennia long—so of course that's what his parents want him to be. But music is in his soul. He'd be miserable as a doctor, and I know his parents would understand that. "What does that have to do with ice cream?"

"It's not the ice cream, exactly," she explains. "It's the sugar."

I give her a look that repeats, *So?*

"His parents were not exactly thrilled by the news."

"That's putting it mildly," Troy adds, returning to a mostly normal, mostly pinky-tan color. "They hit the roof." He shudders. "Literally."

"I still don't—"

"They cursed my taste buds."

That sounds rotten. "What does that mean?"

"Until I agree to become a doctor," he explains, "every time I eat something sweet, it tastes like . . . something *not* sweet."

"That sucks." If this were anything other than White Russian, I'd toss it out in friendship solidarity. But, as I said, it's *White Russian*! I ignore my guilt, trying to be as discreet as possible about my ice-cream ecstasy.

"That's not the worst of it," he says, sounding even more dejected. "They enrolled me in SIPP." When I look confused, he adds, "The Summer Intensive Pre-med Program. Instead of writing songs and practicing, I'll spend all summer in class."

Nicole pats his hand. "You'll get through it, Travatas."

"There's a weeklong anatomy segment," he complains. "Anatomy! We're going to dissect . . . something. I just know it."

"Maybe you can do a virtual dissection or something," I suggest, taking a bite out of the sugar cone. "Nola and I did that in freshman biology."

"Whatever," he says, waving me off. "I don't want to talk about it. What'd you do in camp today?"

Popping the tail end of the cone into my mouth, I reach into my pocket.

"I earned my first merit badge."

I slap the little round patch onto the table.

At first I'd thought Stella was joking. A merit badge? For *not* cracking my skull on the tile? Wow, what an achievement. But then she'd handed this to me and said, "One down, eleven to go."

Just like the ones that covered Nola's Girl Scouts vest in elementary school, this merit badge is round with a thick ring of color surrounding the central picture. In this case, the ring is white, the background is sky blue, and the picture depicts a white whooshy wave of wind.

"*Aerokinesis,*" Troy says. "Cool."

"Did you fly?"

"Not exactly." I pull the badge across the table and slip it back into my pocket. "More like hovered to keep from smashing my head against the courtyard floor."

Nicole and Troy exchange a look. They both say, "The trust fall."

I nod, pretending I'm not crazy proud of myself. But I am.

The study guide says—yes, I finally read it—*aerokinesis* is the ability to move air. In this case, moving enough air under my falling body to hold it suspended. That's pretty darn cool.

"Show us," Nic says.

"What?" My hand is still in my pocket and I smooth my fingers over the edge of the patch. "You want me to trust-fall in here?"

"Nah." She waves off my suggestion. She reaches across the table and grabs the saltshaker, setting it in from of me. "Move this using air."

"I don't think I should—"

"Come on," Troy says. "We want to see what you learned."

I hesitate. What if I can't really control that power? What if I send the salt flying all over the room? That probably mean years of bad luck or something. Or what if I accidentally conjure an entire salt mine? Or if I zap us to the Dead Sea? Or—

"Stop dragging your feet." Nicole points at the shaker. "Go."

"Fine," I say, but not before throwing her an annoyed scowl.

Then I turn my attention to the salt. Keeping in mind what Stella said—I know, right?—I concentrate on trusting the shaker to move. I'm not thinking about the salt or trying to move it or wishing it would move, I just picture it already there. In my mind, the shaker is in front of Nicole. I believe. I trust.

Everything glows. When I blink through the light, I see the little glass shaker slide smoothly down the table. The paper napkin from my cone flutters as the shaker passes.

Nicole catches the shaker as it slides to a stop.

"Nice," she says with a grin.

I release a huge sigh of relief. All I can think is, *It actually worked!* Sure, I'd caught myself before smashing skull to pavement, but it wasn't a conscious effort. This time I actually knew what I was doing. I had a goal. I met that goal.

And nothing blew up!

One step closer to not getting smoted.

"Maybe Goddess Boot Camp is the best thing that could have happened to your powers this summer," Troy says. "Zeus knows it's better than what's happening to *me* this summer."

"At least you're not stuck with Stella and Adara," I reply.

Okay, so Stella's not at the top of my evil-harpy list at the moment. But Adara's holding strong at number one.

"That reminds me," Nicole says. "I might know what happened to the record."

"The one about Phoebe's dad?"

I know, I know. We weren't *supposed* to tell anyone about going into the secret archives. But really, Troy is one of our closest friends. It's not like *he's* going to tell anyone.

"What?" I ask.

"After you ran off to camp," she says, "Philipoulos was so mad about finding it gone that she ranted a bit. She kinda forgot I was there."

"And you didn't try to remind her."

She flashes me a mischievous smile. "She said the only way someone could have slipped past the security of the closet elevator without her knowledge was if they had been a library aide. Anyone who wants a book from the archives has to fill out a request slip. Since Mrs. P is the only librarian on staff, once she has approved their request, she either sends an aide to retrieve the book or goes herself. Which means . . ."

"It had to be a student." I shake my head. "Why would a student want to steal my dad's trial record? Or any record? I mean, it's not like it's breaking news or anything."

"There could be dozens of reasons," Troy says. "Like someone looking for a loophole in an Olympic ruling, for example."

His hazel eyes flick to Nicole.

"Or someone wanting to uncover a secret," she snaps. "Or do a research paper. Or write an article for the *Chronicle*."

The Chronicle? The school newspaper? A puzzle piece falls into place.

"Adara writes for the *Chronicle*." It would be so typical for her to torment me like this. "She could have done it."

"Don't jump to conclusions," Troy says. "Don't accuse her without—"

"She never worked in the library," Nicole interrupts. "But there's another possibility." She pulls a computer printout from her back pocket and sets it in the middle of the table. "Read this."

Troy and I both lean forward to see where she's pointing.

Electronic Catalog and Historiography of Olympus REPORT
Search String: past student employees
Time Frame: 5 years
Query Results: 11 entries

"How did you get this?" Troy asks as I scan the list. "Access to ECHO is insanely restricted. You remember what happened in eighth grade when I tried to change my failing algebra grade." He shudders at the memory. "Sometimes my fingers still tingle when it rains."

"I didn't access the system," Nicole says. "Philipoulos left the printout on her desk when Mr. Sakola asked for help finding the Atlantis collection in the map room. You'd think he was Adonis, the way she dropped everything and—"

My eyes pop out when I see the third name on the list.

"Did you see this?" I point at the third name.

Nicole breaks off and says, "Yeah. I thought that was kind of interesting."

"What?" Troys spins the paper around. After a quick glance, he says, "Holy Hades!"

"Tell me about it." I slump back against the vinyl seat. "And just when I thought we were getting along."

The third name on the list is Stella Petrolas.

As we walk through the village—a little aimlessly because I'm not so eager to go home and face Stella—I know I shouldn't jump to conclusions. Just because Stella *could* have stolen the record doesn't mean she *did*. I mean, she was with me when the note arrived. Even Stella isn't powerful enough to be in two places at once. Of course she could have gotten someone else to leave the note. Or she could have stolen the record, but not have been behind the note. Or she could have nothing to do with anything. Or—

"Let's go to the bakery," Nicole says.

"No thanks," Troy grumbles, looking miserable.

"Come on," Nic says with a smile. "If anyone can make delicious sugar-free treats Lili can."

"Huh-uh," I say, pulling myself out of my Stella ponderings. "Bakery's closed. Griffin and Aunt Lili went to Serifos today to get a fresh stock of berries."

"That's weird," Nicole says. "I could have sworn I saw . . ."

She trails off, her dark blonde eyebrows scrunching down into a frown.

"What?" I ask.

"Nothing." She shakes her head, like she's trying to forget whatever she thought she saw. "Never mind."

"What, Nicole?" I demand. I can tell from the way she's evading that it's bad. A burning ache starts low in my stomach. "Tell me what you saw."

"On my way here"—she gives me an apologetic look—". . . I saw Griffin."

No. That's not possible. He's at the farmer's market on Serifos. That's why we rescheduled our run for this morning. That's why I got up early on my summer vacation. Griffin wouldn't have done that to me for no reason. He wouldn't lie to me. Even when he wanted to hate me when I first got to Serfopoula, he didn't *lie* to me.

But Nicole wouldn't lie to me, either. Not about this.

There must be a reasonable explanation.

Confused, I look up at her. Her blue eyes look sympathetic and a little wary. Nervous.

"What else?" I ask.

She shakes her spiky blonde head, like she doesn't want to tell me. The burning ache takes over my entire stomach, making me regret my hasty consumption of Demetrius's White Russian.

"Just tell me." I take a deep breath. I know she wouldn't be all concerned like this for no reason. "Where did you see him?"

"Going into the bookstore." She closes her eyes and takes a deep breath. "With Adara."

"Oh," I say quietly.

I'm not surprised. After the way he's been behaving—to me and to Adara—this is not completely unexpected. He's been spending as much time with her recently as he has with me. I've been busy the last few weeks—forced into servitude over Stella's graduation, helping get Mom and Damian out the door for their honeymoon, learning how to wield my powers while surrounded by ten-year-olds. He's been busy, too—helping out Aunt Lili in the bakery full-time, getting math tutoring so he can take calculus next year, swapping spit with his ex-girlfriend.

Stepping back from the ledge of conclusion, I make myself consider other possibilities. It could be totally innocent—they could have coincidentally arrived at the bookstore simultaneously and decided to walk in together.

Or, the part of me that still stings from jerky Justin's betrayal screams, it could be totally *not* innocent.

Griffin, I tell myself, *is not Justin.*

"I'm sure it's nothing," I say, trying to sound like I believe it. "They probably just ran into each other."

"Yeah," Troy says.

He's a horrible liar.

"I'm sure you're right," Nicole agrees. "It's nothing."

She's a much better liar, but has much lower tolerance for self-deception. The friend part of her wants to reassure me. The Nicole part of her wants me to be prepared for the reality of the situation.

But whether he ran into Adara or was actually meeting her, the truth is Griffin *did* lie to me. I try to convince myself that he wouldn't. Maybe they got back early. Maybe there was a change of plans. Maybe Aunt Lili decided to go another day. Or alone. Or maybe she didn't want the berries after all. For the moment I am not going to jump to condemn Griffin. After everything we've been through, he deserves the benefit of the doubt.

As we stroll past the bookstore, I resist the urge to look inside. Because with all the mounting evidence, it's getting harder and harder to accept that Griffin and Adara are nothing more than friends. I'm not ready to believe the worst. And the benefit of the doubt is hard to hold on to.

"You never told me you worked at the library," I say when I get home. My voice, cool and collected, echoes in the silent kitchen.

Stella freezes, the refrigerator door open and an ice-filled glass in her hand, for a full five seconds. Straightening, she clears her throat—just like Damian does when he's nervous—and asks, "Should I have?"

I shrug, playing it cool. If I've learned anything from years of Mom headshrinking me, it's that if you want to find out everything, keep your mouth shut. Guilty people love to fill a tense silence.

Grabbing the refrigerator-door handle from her, I pull it wide open. When I lean past her to grab a Gatorade from the stock Hesper keeps in the fridge for me, she says, "I worked there Levels 10 and 11." She fills her glass with water. "I needed some legitimate work experience. I can't exactly put *Hera's Personal Assistant* on my résumé."

I ignore her awkward laugh.

We face off, her leaning against one counter sipping ice water, me leaning against the opposite counter chugging my Gatorade. We just watch each other. I'm waiting for her to crack. Zeus only knows what she's waiting for.

As I drain the last drop of Gatorade, I decide to break the silence. She beats me to it.

"Mrs. Philipoulos called me." Her French-manicured fingers tighten around her glass. "She asked me about the stolen record."

I toss my empty bottle into the recycling bin under the sink. "And?"

"And nothing," she says, looking affronted. "I don't know anything about it. Why would I?"

She looks pretty innocent, but then again Stella's the queen of looking innocent. I can't count the number of times in the last year she's skated on stuff she did. Me? I always get caught. (Not that I ever do anything, of course.)

"But you do know about the secret archives." I don't ask it as a question. "You know how to access them."

"Of course," she says. She finishes her water and sets the glass in the sink. "*Everyone* knows about the 'secret' archives. Mrs. Philipoulos deludes herself into thinking no one knows. It's the worst-kept secret on the island."

That's true. There's still a lot about this island—about this world—that I don't know, and even *I* knew about them.

"You could access them," I repeat. "If you wanted."

"Of course," she replies. At least she didn't deny it. "*If* I wanted. I don't want, and I didn't access. Anyone who's ever worked in the library could access *if* they wanted. Are you going to accuse the entire former payroll staff? Better start with Daddy. He was an aide back in the day. Why don't we give him a call? I'm sure he and Valerie won't mind the interruption on their honeymoon."

I roll my eyes at her melodrama.

Though I haven't got the best record for trusting people, I believe her innocence. Besides, if she'd done it, she'd be gloating about it all over my face. She would still deny it to the authorities, but she'd be taunting me to the ends of the earth.

Where does that leave me? If Stella didn't steal the record, then who?

That brings me back to the list. As soon as I'd seen Stella's name, I'd fixated on that. The rest of the list was pretty much a blur. I need to check out the other names.

"I'll see you at dinner," I say, turning to go to my room and do a little research into my fellow students.

"Phoebe." Something in her voice—something sad—stops me. "Nothing in that record will change what happened. No one can reverse an Olympic decree."

"I know that." I keep my back to her. She doesn't need to see my tears. "But it might give me some answers."

I hear her sigh. "Then I hope you find them. Everyone deserves answers."

Her voice wavers with sympathy, like she understands where I'm coming from. Whatever. She has no idea what I'm going through.

Without responding, I rush to my room. I hate it when she acts like a human—it's so much easier to think of her as a vicious harpy.

At my desk, I pull the folded printout from my back pocket and smooth it out over my closed laptop. I scan the names on the list. Besides Stella, I only recognize three of them.

Katara, Xander

Roukas, Zoe

Martin, Christopher

I can't imagine why any of the three would do this to me. Sure, there are still some—a lot of—lingering ill feelings about me being at the Academy. Students who don't care that I'm one of *them* now, who hate outsiders or runners or Californians or whatever. Or that are resentful because I went from being *nothos* to being a third-generation *hematheos* and therefore pretty powerful and apparently enviable.

But this seems kind of extreme. I mean, it's not like whoever it is won't get in trouble for stealing the record. Damian would probably put them in detention for a year.

Besides, no one on the list seems a likely candidate.

Xander didn't know I existed until camp started, so I doubt he's masterminding the wild-goose chase. Zoe and Christopher are both on the track team. Christopher is one of the nicest guys in school—before I found out about my Nike heritage, he was the only one who would willingly pair up with me in practices. He would never do this. Zoe is one of Adara's minions—translation: she hates me—but she's off the island for the summer, visiting her family in Sweden or Switzerland or something.

I sigh, folding the list back up and slipping it into my desk drawer. No use beating my brain up against a brick wall. I'll have to do some investigating. Maybe Troy and Nicole know something about the other kids on the list. I can ask tomorrow. For tonight I'll do a quick search on the Academy Web site.

I power up my laptop and decide to check e-mail first.

Twelve new messages. And not one of them is spam. Maybe the gods finally developed a functioning spam blocker for the Academy e-mail system.

I quickly skim through my in-box.

To: lostphoebe@theacademy.gr
From: gblake@theacademy.gr
Subject: Training Tomorrow
Phoebes,
Can we run in the morning again tomorrow?
Griff

No explanation. No apologies. No confession that he spent the afternoon at the bookstore with his ex. I take a deep breath. Benefit of the doubt, I tell myself. Benefit of the doubt. I shoot back a quick message saying I'll meet him in the stadium at eight in the morning. I'm sure there is a perfectly rational reason.

I click to the next message.

To: lostphoebe@theacademy.gr
From: granolagrrl@pacificpark.us
Subject: Good News
The grant committee reconvened early. No decision yet, but I'll find out sooner rather than later whether I get it.
Peace and love,
Nola

Crossing my fingers and toes, I send a silent plea that the grant committee gives Nola her research grant. Just the thought of hanging out for a couple of weeks—instead of the couple of days we've spent together since I left L.A.—makes me forget all the craziness of the day.

If Nola comes to visit, then all will be right with the world.

Or half right anyway. If she and Cesca both come it will be perfect.

To: lostphoebe@theacademy.gr
From: princesscesca@pacificpark.us
Subject: Paris Is Calling
Hey hot stuff. Just a quick e-mail to update my sched. I've got to be in Paris, like, yesterday. I'm on a plane tomorrow and have to report to work at six the next day—that's six in the *morning*! Ugh. I'm busy

packing. Don't know when I'll be able to e-mail, but I'll get in touch as soon as I can. Want anything from the city of lights?

XOXO Cesca

Cesca is even less of a morning person than I am, but I know that she'll do anything to spend the summer traipsing around after fashion designers in her personal holy city. One day her designs will grace the covers of every major fashion magazine.

To: lostphoebe@theacademy.gr
From: valeriepetrolas@hotmail.com
Subject: We've Got Mail
Phoebola,
Sorry we haven't called. International rates from Bangkok are phenomenally expensive. But e-mail is not. They have a business center in the hotel lobby, so here I am. We arrived safely and will stay in Bangkok for two more days before setting out on the guided tour of the rest of the country. We're actually going to be in Phuket for their international marathon. We'll get you a souvenir t-shirt.

Is everything going alright at home? You and Stella haven't strangled each other, have you? How were your first days of boot camp? Make any new friends?

I know that controlling your powers is an unfamiliar challenge, but you are the strongest, most dedicated, strong-willed young woman I've ever known. You have your father's drive to succeed, and that more than anything else will see you through this trial. I have absolute faith in you.

Damian and I are on our way to a traditional Thai dance performance, a style called *khon*. I will write more when I can. Call if you need anything.

Have fun and don't murder your stepsister.

Love,

Mom

That's pretty cool that they'll get to see an international marathon. I wish I could go. Before we moved to Serfopoula, I never had a burning desire to be anywhere but Southern California. Now I wish I could go everywhere. It's like if being in Greece changed my perspective on the world so much—for the better—then I can only imagine how different I would be if I saw even more of it.

I send Mom a quick reply—mainly because I think she'll brave the cost of a phone call if I don't. My mind is such a mess right now I know she'd pick up on it and the last thing I need is her turning into therapist Mom from thousands of miles away.

I don't want to open the next e-mail, but know I should.

To: lostphoebe@theacademy.gr

From: cheergirl@theacademy.gr

Subject: Boot Camp Update

Greetings Campers

PROPER CAMP ATTIRE: Please wear closed-toe shoes and long pants every day. NO SHORTS or SANDALS!!! This is for your own protection.

Tomorrow's boot camp will be something SPECIAL! Meet in front of the maintenance shed at the north end of the quad at 10 A.M.! Late-comers will be left behind and this is a day you will not want to miss!

~ Adara ~

I roll my eyes. Besides her overuse of exclamation points and her tendency to yell, the idea that we're doing "something special" in camp tomorrow is not exciting. It's terrifying.

Next is an administrative message from Ms. T, the Level 13 coordinator.

To: Level 13 Students

From: tyrovolas@theacademy.gr

Subject: Upcoming School Year

Attention all returning Level 13 students:

Summer is not too early to begin planning your academic future. You will meet in individual sessions with your assigned adviser at the end of August, but I encourage you to review the course catalog and make a list of those you would like to schedule. Because many Level 13 classes have restricted enrollment, you should also list second and third choices for every period. Any advance preparation will make your advising session go far smoother.

I appreciate your efforts in this endeavor.

Tanya Tyrovolas

Level 13 Coordinator

Professor of Literature

The Academy

Serfopoula, Greece

Ms. T is a bit of a nutcase. She wears togas to school and I think she's a strong advocate of reinstating trial by combat—as in *gladiatorial* combat, which was banned in the sixth century. I make a reminder in my Academy calendar to look at the course catalog before August. The last thing I want is to spend my (second) senior year enrolled in classes I hate.

I skim through the next few messages.

An automated system message reminding students that Academy e-mail is rigorously scanned and violators of the terms of use will be required to take a forty-hour "Responsible Electronic Communications" course.

Three e-mails from school clubs, encouraging new members to join now to beat the fall rush—yeah, like Mock Government is going to be turning them away at the door.

An e-mail from the maintenance staff, asking students to remove personal items from lockers before the buildingwide clean-out next week.

The last e-mail—with no sender and no subject—piques my curiosity.

To: lostphoebe@theacademy.gr

From: [Blocked]

Subject: [No Subject]

Curious about the contents of the missing Olympic record?

Be in the courtyard at midnight on Tuesday.

Come alone.

My heart starts racing. My mind starts racing. So whoever sent me the note already *knew* the record was missing? Then why did they send the note? Is this the same person who stole it? Or do they know who did?

What if they are just trying to mess with me? Or hurt me? It wouldn't be the first time someone at the Academy went out of their way to make me look and feel like an idiot. Would I be totally stupid to agree to this meeting?

And if I don't, will I ever find out what really happened to Dad?

CHAPTER 7

VISIOCRYPTION

SOURCE: HADES

The ability to hide, mask, or cloak an object. Duration of effect and size of object affected varies depending on strength of power. Effect is temporary and does not affect the physical characteristics of the object. (See *Visiomutation* for permanent changes of appearance.)

DYNAMOTHEOS STUDY GUIDE © Stella Petrolas

WHEN I WALK THROUGH THE TUNNEL and out onto the stadium field the next morning, Griffin is waiting for me next to the soccer goal—sure, in Greece they call it football, but my dad played *football*. The sport with a round, black-and-white ball will always be soccer to me. Griff smiles that heart-melting smile, gives me a quick kiss, and says, "I missed you, *kardia tis kardias mou*."

Until that moment I have every intention of letting the whole Griffin-and-Adara-in-the-bookstore thing go. Not every guy is a cheating jerk like Justin.

But when he says he missed me, I wonder, *Did he really?*

I can't stop myself from asking, "How was the trip to Serifos?"

"Oh," he says. "We had to reschedule. The freezer malfunctioned and flooded the cellar. Aunt Lili and I spent the morning rearranging the stockroom."

So he *hadn't* left the island yesterday. "Is that why we're running in the morning again?"

"Didn't I say that?" He bends over, reaching for his toes.

No, he didn't say that.

Joining him in the stretch, I ask, "What did you do in the afternoon?"

I feel like the Inquisition.

He's not avoiding eye contact, I tell myself. He can't exactly look me in the eye when he's hanging upside down and pulling himself into deeper extension.

"I stopped by the bookstore." He spreads his feet and twists to reach for one ankle. "Wanted to see if they had anything on endurance conditioning and nutrition."

Of course it was something innocent—he was researching our training.

I smile as I mimic his stretching, mentally whipping myself. Clearly, I need to get a handle on that jealousy monster—which Nicole insists has red eyes, not green. Sometimes I wonder how she knows so much about mythological beasts. Other times I don't want to know.

"Did they?" I lift my foot behind me and grab my ankle, stretching my quads.

"No." He smiles and says, "But Iona said they would order some for us."

Why am I so eager to assume the worst about Griff?

As the daughter of a psychiatrist, I do *not* go in for the therapy thing. After a lifetime of psychoanalysis, I'm immune. But I'm starting to think that maybe I need some help on my trust issues. I mean, I shouldn't be so quick to doubt Griffin. Especially not after what we went through to get together.

We're fated by an oracle, after all.

If the prophecy says Griffin will "find his match in a daughter of victory"—aka the goddess Nike, aka my great-grandmother—then our relationship, our future is secure, right?

The red-eyed monster needs to take a hike.

"So what's our training plan for today?" he asks, interrupting my self-exploration.

I give him a wicked grin. "Steps."

"Excuse me?"

I nod in the direction of the stadium stands. "We're going to run steps."

He looks warily up at the stands.

The stadium is a smaller version of the Roman Colosseum—or maybe the Colosseum is a bigger version of the Academy stadium?—but it's still several stories high. From field level to the top row of bench seats is probably around one hundred steps. I don't know what Griffin is worried about. This is nothing. It's my dream to run the steps of the Eiffel Tower, the Statue of Liberty, and the Empire State Building. Stadium steps are no big deal.

"All right," he says, without enthusiasm. "Let's do it."

After a quick four-lap warm-up and another round of stretching, we tackle the steps. There are ninety-six, to be exact, and I know this because we run them a dozen times. I count them aloud each time.

As we turn around for our final climb, I begin counting down. "Ninety-six, ninety-five, ninety-four . . ."

"How many more?" Griffin gasps.

"Ninety, eighty-nine, eighty-eight," I pant, keeping my count. "Last one."

"Thank the gods," Griffin gasps as we keep climbing.

I manage a smile that probably looks more like a wince. Griffin doesn't notice—he's too busy trying not to die.

"Sixty-three, sixty-two . . ." I manage, though my lungs and my quads and my everything are burning. Every last muscle in my body is screaming, desperately begging me to stop this insanity, to just drop down and die like a normal person.

But I'm not a normal person, I tell my body. *I'm a runner. Pain is my game.* All this bodily rebellion tells me I've let my endurance go. Cutting back on my running time for the last few months to work on controlling my powers has made my running suffer—and it hasn't done wonders for my powers, either.

A wave of endorphins washes over me, bringing that familiar feeling of invincibility. With crystal clarity, I know that somehow—I'm not sure exactly how, but somehow—everything will work out. I'll get a hold on my powers. I'll keep my race training on track. And I'll learn to trust Griffin . . . somehow.

A girl can't spend her whole life suffering the aftershocks of one bad boyfriend.

"When we reach the top," Griffin wheezes between sucking breaths, "just push me over the edge."

"Not on your life." I wince-smile again. "Nineteen, eighteen, seventeen . . ."

He grunts, but keeps taking step after step.

We're so close.

The muscle burn is overwhelming. I concentrate on the lactic-acid buildup in my quads, embracing the pain and knowing that it means my muscles are trying to work more efficiently. Trying to keep up with what I'm forcing them to do. I'll pay them back later with a long soak in a hot bath.

"Three," Griffin says, probably trying to hurry the countdown.

"Two." I can almost feel the recovery that will begin as soon as we reach the peak.

"One." He bursts up onto the top level of the stadium, raising his fisted hands in the air at our success . . . and then dropping them immediately when the exhaustion overtakes the thrill.

"We did it!" I join him and stop long enough to squeeze a quick hug around his waist.

"Let's never do this again," he gasps.

"Never again," I agree as he turns and starts the final descent. Then I smile. "Until next week."

I can hear his groan from a dozen steps away.

Before following him to the stadium floor, I hesitate, casting a glance out over the parapet to appreciate the view from this far up.

The island of Serfopoula stretches several miles to the east, covered in barren rocky patches and thick pine forest, interspersed with stretches of shrubby plains. To the north, a lush green valley peeks out between rolling hills. As I turn to descend one last time—for today, anyway—I think about how little of the island I've actually experienced. Since the school and the village are on the west end, I've only really seen that part. The only beaches I've run are on this end. I wonder if the beaches on the eastern shore are the same silky white sand?

"I think I'm going to die," Griffin says as we reach the field and he collapses on the grass. "No. I think I *want* to die."

"Don't be silly," I say, pacing a circle around his carcass. "Besides, we have to cool down."

"I can't move."

"You have to." I focus on my breathing as I reach down and grab his wrist, tugging him back to his feet. "You won't be able to walk tomorrow if you don't."

Despite his groans, he follows me into a jog around the track.

After one lap at a casual pace—and on flat ground—my breathing has almost returned to normal and the burn in my quads has ebbed to a comfortable ache. Trust me, after this many years of running, a dull ache *is* comfortable. It's comforting.

"If I didn't know you adored me," he says as we start our second lap, "I'd think you were trying to kill me."

"Just imagine what I would do to someone I *don't* like."

Someone like Adara.

No. I shake my head. I will not let her sneak into my thoughts, into this time with Griffin. My time with him is limited enough this summer, between his job and my camp and the looming test and whoever is sending me on a wild-goose chase for the missing record of my dad's trial.

Why can't anything on this island be simple? At Pacific Park, the most dramatic thing that ever happened was a social nobody winning homecoming queen. One year at the Academy and suddenly I'm a goddess, dating a real-life hero, and hunting for a Mount Olympus record book.

"What do you know about the secret archives?" I ask absently.

Griffin stumbles. "The what?"

"The secret archives of Mount Olympus," I repeat. "Come on, I know they're not really a secret."

"Oh, *those* secret archives."

"Are there other secret archives?"

"Not that I know of." He laughs. "What do *you* know about the secret archives?"

"Not as much as I'd like." I shrug as we round lap two. "I know they contain the records of Mount Olympus and the remains of the Library of Alexandria."

"Really?"

"And they have seriously limited access."

"I don't know much more," he says. "What do you want to know?"

There are so many possible questions. How far back do the records go? What else do the archives hold? Who files the documents? But there is only one question I care about.

"I want to know how someone would steal one of the records—"

Griffin stumbles again. "You don't want to—"

"—and why they would steal the record of my dad's trial."

"Someone stole that?" he asks as we slow to a walk. "How do you know?"

"Because when Nicole and I went looking for it yesterday, it was gone."

"So that's how . . ." He shakes his head, scowling, and then starts over. "That's how you knew about the archives."

I'm pretty sure that's not what he started to say.

"I don't know why someone would steal your dad's record," he replies. "There's a rumor about a secret entrance to the library. If someone wanted to get in and out of the secret archives unnoticed, that might be how."

Great. A rumor of a secret entrance to the secret archives. How is that supposed to help me? I feel like I've been dropped into the middle of a Harry Potter book. Next, some evil genius is going to be plotting to kill me.

We finish our cooldown laps and make our way through the tunnel to the campus quad. As we reemerge into the morning sun, I hang back a step to admire Griffin in his fresh-from-a-workout glory. His nicely tanned arms and legs are glistening with sweat, the moisture catching the low-angle sun like a mirror rippling with every move of his lean muscles.

When he realizes I'm not at his side, Griffin turns, catches me ogling, and his mouth spreads in that cocky grin I love so much.

"Enjoying the view?" he teases.

"Maybe." I saunter up to him, then—unable to keep up the coy act—wrap my arms around his neck and tug him close until our foreheads touch. "You have a problem with me looking?"

Shaking his head slowly against mine, he hums, *"Huh-uh."*

Then his hand cups the back of my neck and he pulls my mouth the few inches to meet his. I love the feel of his soft lips against mine. Nine months of kissing him whenever I want and I still can't get enough.

I slip my arms farther around his neck, stretching myself into him and up into the kiss. When he drops his hands to press against my lower back, shivers race down my spine and over my exhausted muscles. He's mine, all mine. No one else gets to kiss him like this.

An image—a memory—flashes into my mind. Of Griffin. Of me watching him across the crowded school cafeteria while he is locked in exactly this embrace. With Adara.

I jerk back.

It feels like a bucket of ice water emptied over me.

Removing myself from Griffin's arms, I take a step back.

"I, uh . . ." The stabbing pain around my heart is worse than any lactic-acid buildup. I know it isn't fair, holding something from the past against him. But is it really in the past? I can't think. I need to get away from him so my brain can return to seminormal function. "Gotta go."

"Yeah," he says, breathing heavy. "You'd better hurry if you're getting a shower before camp."

Right. Camp.

I glance down at my sweat-soaked I RUN THEREFORE I AM CRAZY

T-shirt and shorts. For a second I consider going as is—and taking every opportunity to brush my stinky self up against Adara. But then I remember my dignity—and her e-mail last night about not wearing shorts. As much as I'd like to completely ignore her instructions, I don't want to wind up bit by a snake or a hydra or some other creepy-crawly just to spite her. With my luck, today would be fight-a-mythological-monster day.

"You're right," I say before I get sucked into those bright blue eyes for a lifetime or two. "I need a shower." Pressing a quick kiss to his mouth, I ask, "Maybe you can come by after you get back from Serifos?"

"I'll have to help Aunt Lili put everything away." He gives me a lopsided grin. "But I'll try to steal away. Why don't we meet at the dock at seven for a sunset walk on the beach."

"We could always fit in another training run," I tease.

Griffin groans. "Are you trying to kill me?"

I glance at my watch and realize just how late I am.

"Of course not," I say, backing away across the quad. "If you were dead, who would I train with?"

∽∽∽∽∽

"Today we are going to do a team exercise called Navigator," Stella explains as I try to slip unnoticed into the group assembled behind the maintenance shed. She glares at me. I'm not *that* late. A minute or two. Five at the most.

"We have divided you into four teams—three teams of three and one team of four." Adara throws me a glare of her own, like I intentionally ruined her even division of teams. She gives me too little credit for inventiveness—like giving her an odd number of campers is the worst thing I could think of—and too much credit for interest in her. I have better things to do with my mental faculties than make her life miserable. It may be a bonus effect, but I have plenty of my own miseries to worry about.

"Each team will be assigned a supervisor, either Miss Orivas, Stella, Xander, or myself." She flips over a page on her clipboard and reads aloud. "The teams are as follows . . ."

As Adara reads the names on the list of teams, I glance around at the ten-year-olds. They are all dutifully wearing pants and either sneakers or hiking shoes. She lists the members of the first three teams, those supervised by Stella, Adara, and Miss Orivas. The girls line up behind their assigned leader.

"The remaining four campers—Tansy, Muriel, Gillian, and Phoebe," Adara says, with an extra-sugary-sweet grin at me, "are assigned to Xander."

"Each supervisor will now explain the exercise," Stella says. "The teams are not allowed further communication until Navigator is over."

As Stella, Adara, and Miss Orivas lead their girls in separate directions for the debriefing or whatever, Xander doesn't move from the spot where he's comfortably leaning against the maintenance shed. My three teammates settle into the grass at his feet.

He glances at me and raises a brow.

The rebel thing doesn't do it for me. I move to stand behind the older girl—I think her name is Tansy—and cross my arms. As if I'm going to sit at his feet.

"Navigator," Xander begins, "is an exercise in strategy, teamwork, and most of all, trust."

Again with the trust thing? We've already done that.

He pushes away from the shed and jerks some pink papers from his back pocket. As he hands them to Gillian he says, "Hidden in the woods behind us are a dozen team flags. Three for each team."

Tansy twists around to hand me one of the papers. It's an odd-looking map, with a series of twisting trails, bushy kindergarten-looking trees, and a dozen *X*s marked in evenly distributed spots. There's a map legend at the bottom and the *I*s are dotted with little hearts. Adara's handiwork, no doubt.

Although, with Stella's crazy crush on rebel boy, she might have sunk to heart-doodling, too.

"Are we to find the flags?" the third girl on my team—what was her name?—asks.

"Let him finish, Muriel," Gillian says.

"Yes, Muriel," Xander says, not a flicker of emotion in his lavender eyes, "we will find the flags. The trick is finding the *right* flags."

Whatever that's supposed to mean.

Fifteen minutes later, I'm traipsing through the woods behind the ten-year-olds, with Xander bringing up the rear. This is the dumbest game I've ever played. Like I don't have better things to do than hunt for stupid flags in a stupid forest. I could be visiting Serifos with Griffin or helping Nicole with her research project or figuring out who is sending me mysterious messages.

"You're falling behind."

I don't have to glance over my shoulder to know Xander is right behind me. "And your point is?"

"This is a team effort." Twigs crack beneath our steps. "Maybe, since running is an individual sport, you're not familiar with the concept."

Like he has a clue. Sure, each race is an individual runner against other individual runners, but there's also the overall competition. Every race is worth team points. A different number of points for each scoring place—the number of scoring places determined by how many runners are in the race. If there are thirty runners, then usually the first three finishers get points for their team. These points accumulate over the course of the meet, and the *team* with the highest total at the end wins the overall.

I'm never racing only for myself.

But I don't expect him to understand. Stomping harder across the forest floor, I retort, "And just what teams have you been on?"

"I never said I was a team player."

"Then why are you here?" I ask. He seems more like the type to take a solo motorcycle trip across China than to spend his summer babysitting tweens and *dynamotheos* rejects. "You're not exactly oozing enthusiasm."

"Let's just say I owe Petrolas a favor."

"Because Damian readmitted you after your expulsion?"

I slap a hand over my mouth. The question slipped out before I knew it was coming. I totally want to know, of course, but I totally *don't* want to get zapped to Siberia. Xander definitely gives off a cross-me-and-you'll-never-be-heard-from-again vibe.

I brace myself for subarctic temperatures.

"Not exactly," he says as we reach a wide spot in the trail—if the barely visible, less dense path is a trail. Picking up his pace, he passes me. "And I didn't say *which* Petrolas."

I'm left watching his back as he catches up with my team. He has definitely cornered the market on enigma. I hope Stella goes for the deeply layered type.

"I found one!"

The piercing little-girl shriek echoes through the woods. I follow the sound of yelps and giggles to where my team and Xander have gathered. They're pointing at a white flag hanging from a low tree branch.

"This is one of ours," Tansy insists. "I'm sure of it."

"Remember," Xander says, "if you choose the wrong flag, then you'll lose a point and give the rightful team a two-point bonus."

Note that rebel boy said "you," not "we." And he thinks *I* don't understand the team concept.

Though no one appears interested in my opinion, I evaluate the flag.

According to Xander's instructions, all the flags on the course look identical. White. We can't trust appearances to know which one is ours. As soon as we touch the flag, it will change colors—to black if it belongs to us, to red, blue, or yellow if it belongs to Stella, Adara, or Miss Orivas. But we can't know for sure until we touch it.

"You have to *feel* the flag." Xander leans casually against a tree. "See beyond the surface." He looks at me. "If you can."

I scowl at him. In a perfect world, the tree would be swarming with ants.

Maybe if I concentrate, I can—

"I think we should grab it," Gillian says, taking a step toward the tree.

Out of the corner of my eye I see her reaching . . . for a *red* flag.

"Wait!" I dive in front of her, pushing her hand out of the way inches before she could touch the still-white flag.

"What are you doing?" Gillian cries.

Muriel crosses her arms over her chest and glares at me.

"What, Phoebe?" Tansy asks, seeming truly interested in my opinion. From the murderous looks on Gillian and Muriel's faces and the total disinterest on Xander's, she's the only one who wants to hear what I have to say. "Don't you think this is our flag?"

I glance at the flag again. It's still white. I have no reason to think Gillian's wrong—especially since *I'm* the one with the defective powers. She's probably decades ahead of me in the whole powers-control thing. But for that instant I was so sure it—

Red. For another split second the flag was red.

"No." I shake my head. "This isn't ours. This flag is red."

"Whatever," Gillian says, reaching for the flag again.

Tansy gasps. "I see it, too."

Gillian and Muriel stare at her like she's betrayed them.

She points at the flag. "Look."

They both turn and squint. Gillian's mouth drops. Muriel huffs and stomps away. "Let's go find our flags." She ducks under a pine branch. "I am *not* losing to Tressa Boyd."

Gillian hurries after her. As Xander passes me, he says, "Nice catch, Castro."

I just keep blinking, not quite believing what I just did. When I looked at the flag, I saw the white mask or whatever. When I was thinking about something else, though, only catching sight in my peripheral vision, I could see the true color.

"That was amazing," Tansy says, her voice laced with a sense of awe. "You didn't even have to concentrate or anything."

No, I didn't. In fact, concentrating made it worse.

Stella's exercise the other night proved that my powers come from my mind. But how am I supposed to control them if focusing doesn't help?

"We'd better hurry up," Tansy says. "I bet Gillian tries to grab the wrong flag again. If you're not there to stop her, we'll lose for sure."

I let Tansy lead me up the path, but my mind is still thinking about my powers. And how I only have less than two weeks to fig- ure out how to control them when *trying* to control them sends them out of control.

At this point, I really shouldn't be surprised by being tossed into such a vicious circle. Try to control my powers, and they go berserk. Train more, control less. Stay on at the Academy to learn how to use my powers, but be forced to pass a powers test first. Lately, my whole life is one big exercise in contradiction.

"Congratulations, Phoebe," Stella says when camp breaks up for the day. "Xander says you found two of your team's flags, and saved them from choosing three wrong ones."

I shrug. It's not like I actually *did* something to succeed. "No big."

"It is a big," she insists. "Most *neos* are lucky to find one. They almost never identify enemy flags. You've earned your second merit badge. "

She hands me another round patch. This one has a red outer ring, a black background, and the center picture looks like a magician's wand with little sparks coming out the end. I guess it has something to do with masking appearances or making something invisible. Making the colored flags look white.

Big whoop.

I glance around to make sure everyone else is gone. I don't want to get caught confessing to the evil stepsister.

"But what good does it do me?" I ask when I'm sure we're alone. "If I try to use my powers, they go wacky. It's only when I'm not thinking about it that they come out right."

"Hmm." Stella taps a French-manicured finger on her lips. "There has to be a way to reverse that. Or at least harness it."

I can see the gears turning, her mind working to figure out the solution.

"Maybe you're overthinking, overanalyzing," she suggests. "There's an exercise designed to—"

"Forget it," I say, walking away. I'm so not up for Stella's full attention right now. After six hours of indirect powers usage in the company of ten-year-olds—except, as I found out, Tansy . . . she's twelve—my mind is fried. "I can't think about this anymore right now."

"We can try that exercise tonight," she calls out.

Following the path around the quad, I pass the girls' dorm. I'm thankful I don't have to live there. Sharing my bathroom with Stella is bad enough. I can't imagine sharing with an entire floor full of girls. Like Adara. I feel sorry for Nicole—she is so not the slumber-party type, but she's on the same floor as the cheer queen and three of her cheer minions.

As Nicole puts it, she's trapped in cheerland. This is her fourth summer in the dorms. Maybe she's built up a defense against Aphrodite's descendants.

Or, knowing Nicole, maybe she's placed some kind of curse on her door so they can't get into her room.

I'll have to ask her.

Detouring from the path, I decide to see if she's home. Maybe she can shed some light on the anonymous e-mail.

Her room is at the end of the first floor, with a great view out over the quad. Even if I didn't know which one was hers, I'd be able to guess—it's the only one with a sign that says KNOCK AT YOUR OWN PERIL just below a skull and crossbones. Braving the warning—but making sure to knock on the door itself, and *not* the sign—I rap my knuckles on the smooth wood surface.

No response. If she were here, I'd at least get a threatening "Who is it?"

I'm not ready to go home and I don't want to be alone. Classes should be out for the day. Maybe Troy is in his room.

I head back out and toward the boys' dorm and climb the front steps and the two flights of stairs to his third-floor room. My quads cry out a little at the climb, reminding me that recovery time is a good thing. When I reach the room with a giant foam guitar on the door, I knock. Three seconds later, Troy pulls it open.

"Phoebe," he says with huge smile. "What are you doing here?"

"Camp just ended," I say. "I was heading home and thought I'd stop by."

"Get your butt in here, Castro," Nicole barks.

Troy swings the door wide so I can see Nic lounging on the beanbag in the corner. She's just sliding a big leather book into her messenger bag.

She waves me in. "We've been waiting for you to show up."

"What's up?" I ask.

"I don't know what Nic's doing here," he teases. When she casts a scowl his way, he grabs the guitar off his bed and sets in on the stand next to his desk. "I was just about to play for some stress relief. My brain was not made for organic chemistry."

"I don't want to interrupt." I do, actually, but it seems way rude to say that. Even if I'm desperate for some reprieve from my own troubles.

"No worries." He drops into his dorm-issue desk chair and motions me to the bed. "You're stress relief, too."

"Thanks," I say, sinking onto his black-and-white-checkered comforter. "I don't feel much like stress relief today."

"Hard day at camp?" Nicole asks, pulling a bag of butterscotch candies out of her bag. She thrusts the bag in my direction.

Troy growls a little and frowns at the candy.

I lean over and take one. "Yes. No. I don't know." I twist open the cellophane wrapper. "It's more than camp, I guess."

Popping the butterscotch between my lips, I let the smoothly sweet taste melt over my tongue.

"Like what?" Nic asks.

Oh, everything. It's that I can only control my powers when I'm not trying to. It's that I'm afraid my boyfriend is getting back with his ex—or that I'm having an overreaction of jealousy. It's that I'm stuck at home with Stella, with her taking me on as her pet project. It's that I'm suddenly doubting what I learned about my dad's death, my boyfriend's loyalty, and my own sanity. It's a million things and nothing.

Not that I say any of that. Don't need to expose my friends to the insane ramblings of my brain. They might never recover.

"Like this." I lift one hip and pull two pieces of paper from my back pocket.

Nicole snatches them from my hand.

After unfolding them, she says, "They're blank."

"I know." I slide the butterscotch against my cheek so I can talk. "They're not *supposed* to be blank. They're *supposed* to be e-mail printouts." I slip the butterscotch back onto my tongue and mutter, "Thtupid, curthed e-mails."

"They wouldn't print?" Troy asks.

I shake my head. When I received the second e-mail last night,

145

almost identical to the first, I wanted a printout so I could I analyze them. Maybe find a clue to who sent them.

Forty-seven attempts later, all I had was blank paper.

"Huh." Troy's brows scrunch together. "Who were they from?"

"The same person who sent the note," Nicole suggests.

"Probably." Unable to resist, I crunch the butterscotch. Someday my teeth will be dust. "The sender's address was blocked."

"Blocked?" Troy's eyes get all wide. "This was to your Academy e-mail?" When I nod, he shakes his head. "The Academy e-mail system doesn't allow blocked senders."

I shrug. As if I can change what happened.

"Show me." He leaps up from his desk chair and waves me over. "Log on to your e-mail."

With a heavy sigh, I push off the bed. It's not that I don't want to find out who sent the message, and how they managed to block the sender *and* keep it from printing. I am just running low on motivation.

When I'm slow to move, Troy takes my shoulders, urges me into the chair, and shoves me closer to the desk. Grabbing the mouse, I click the Academy e-mail logo and enter my user name and password.

"See." I point at the blocked messages, still at the top of my inbox.

Troy leans over my shoulder, squinting at the screen. "I can't believe it. Academy e-mail is impenetrable. No one can bypass the security system without major repercussions."

"What about last year," I ask, "when Griffin messed with my e-mail? Every time I deleted his message a new one popped up."

"That's different." Troy rubs a hand back and forth over his short hair. "Anyone can create a simple hack on their own computer to automatically resend a message. But this messes with the Academy server. It's impossible."

"Maybe," I say, thinking, *Clearly not*. "But that doesn't change the fact that—"

"Let's take this to Urian," Nic says. "He'll figure it out."

"She's right. The kid's a genius." Troy jerks the desk chair back, with me in it. "Let's go."

He hurries out into the hall. Nicole shrugs, like we both know he's overreacting, but follows him through the door. When I get into the hall, I see Troy knocking on a door three rooms down. When there's no answer, he rolls his eyes and knocks again, this time with a *knock-knock . . . knock . . . knock-knock-knock* pattern.

"Password?" a muffled voice says through the door.

"Chimera."

No answer.

"Shoot," Troy whispers. "That was yesterday's password." To the door, he says, "Scylla's strait."

Nicole rolls her eyes.

The door swings open silently.

"Don't," Troy whispers through clenched teeth, "laugh."

We walk into a room straight out of *Star Wars*. Complete with crossed lightsabers over the desk, black curtains blocking out the window, and a life-size Han Solo cutout in the corner.

A giggle bubbles its way to the surface. Troy cuts me a harsh look and I stifle my humor. But seriously, a life-size Han Solo?

"State your purpose?"

Turning toward the voice, I see a short, dark-haired boy pushing the door closed. I can't tell for sure—like I said, the window is blacked out and the only light in the room is coming from the glow of a computer monitor—but I don't think I know him.

"Academy e-mail," Troy says.

"Familiar," the dark-haired boy says, leaving his post at the door and sliding into the chair in front of his computer. "Situation?"

"Blocked sender." Troy moves farther into the room and sits on the unmade bed, on the edge nearest the desk.

"Impossible." Dark-haired boy clicks rapidly on his keyboard.

"*Not* impossible," Troy says, leaning forward so he can see the monitor. "I've seen it."

Nicole leans close to my ear and whispers, "Urian's a little psycho, but he knows computers better than anyone."

Dark-haired boy stops typing. "Additional inconsistencies?"

"The message won't print."

Dark-haired boy grunts and starts typing faster than ever. Images flash across the monitor at warp speed.

I feel like I've entered nerd-ville.

I stick to my spot just inside the door. From what I can see in the flickering light, the rest of the room looks like a hurricane, tornado, *and* tsunami took turns messing with the contents. I'm suddenly very glad I had to wear pants and closed-toe shoes for camp today. Who knows what's living in those piles.

"Access codes?" dark-haired boy finally asks.

"Phoebe," Troy says, "tell Urian your user name and password."

"No way," I say. I don't know this guy. I've read about those identity thieves who hijack your e-mail and use it to send spam about
discount prescription drugs and pirated computer programs.

"Urian's all right," Nicole says.

I stand my ground. "I don't know him."

"Phoebe, this is Urian Nacus." She nods at the dark-haired boy.
"Urian, Phoebe Castro."

Urian spins in his chair faster than an Olympic sprinter. "Castro?" he asks, brows raised. "The *aponikos*?"

"The what?" I asked, thinking I might need to get offended.

"Descendant of Nike," Troy says quickly, as if he can sense I'm
upset.

Urian leaps to his feet and bows politely. "A pleasure." Flashing
me a smarmy smile, he takes my hand—which I *didn't* offer—and
kisses my knuckles.

"Uh, thanks," I say, retrieving my fingers.

I glare at Troy over Urian's head. What has he gotten me into?

"Please," Urian says, waving at the flickering computer screen.
"Key in your user name and password. Your access codes shall remain your own."

After giving Troy one more who-is-this-guy? look, I plop into the
desk chair, and access my e-mail. A split second later, my in-box is
on the screen.

"That was *fast*," I say, impressed.

"I installed a signal enhancer," Urian says, leaning over my shoulder to read the screen. "It quadrupled my connection speed."

Figures. He probably spends all his time downloading episodes of *Hercules* and *Xena*.

Before Urian the Curious can read all my other messages, I click open the blocked e-mail.

"There it is," I say, nodding at the screen.

Urian studies it for a minute. His bushy eyebrows keep scrunching and unscrunching, as if he's physically processing with his forehead. Weird.

"May I?" he asks, nodding at the chair.

I shrug and get up.

"First, I need to access the Academy mail server," he says. A new window opens up on the computer. "The original file might still contain the metadata from the—" He smacks his mouse down on the desk. "Blast! It's blocked, as well." More furious typing. "The source file didn't even log the originating IP address."

Before my eyes permanently roll back in my head from trying to follow the computer-speak, I ask, "What does that mean?"

"In plain English?" He glances up at me. "Whoever sent this is very, very smart."

"Or very, very powerful," Troy says. "Bypassing Academy e-mail security is anything but easy."

"True." Urian squints at the screen. "This isn't a simple hack job. It's going to take me a while."

"Sometime before midnight Tuesday would be nice," I say. "I'd like to know who I'm meeting."

"You're not seriously going?" Troy asks.

As if there was any doubt?

"Of course I'm going," I say. "What other choice do I have?"

"Um . . . *not* going."

"Troy, I have to find out what happened to my dad."

"We *know* what happened to your dad. He got smoted. End of story."

"Not," I snap, "end of story. At least, not anymore. I can't just let this go."

"Fine." Troy crosses his arms over his chest. "I'll go with you."

"Chill, Travatas," Nicole says. Then to me she says, "I think what Tarzan here is trying to say is that whoever pulled off this e-mail stunt—and snuck into the secret archives—has to be pretty powerful. And pretty devious. You shouldn't meet this person alone."

"No." I can't believe she's siding with him. "The e-mail says I have to come alone. I'm not going to blow this."

Troy glares at me, looking like he *really* wants to say something more. But, instead, he turns to Urian and asks, "Can you find out before then?"

"One hundred and twenty hours, give or take?" He looks like he's crunching numbers in his head—my brain hurts just thinking about it—and then finally says, "That's cutting it close. Fifty-fifty chance."

"Great," I say.

"I copied the source file into my e-mail account," Urian says. "But I may still need to access your—"

"No way." He may be helping me out, but I still only met him like two minutes ago. Besides, a girl needs her privacy.

"Not a problem," he says with a grin. "My computer recorded your keystrokes. If I need access, I have your codes."

"Great," I say, less enthusiastically than before.

"Let's meet here on Tuesday night," Nicole suggests. "Eleven o'clock?"

"Excellent," Urian says.

"Fine by me," I say, still annoyed at Troy. Since when did he become my guardian and protector?

"See you Tuesday," Troy says as we leave.

"The countdown has begun," Urian returns.

Geek melodrama. I roll my eyes.

"And, Urian," Nicole says, "you might try doing laundry once in a while."

As we step into the hall, she pulls the door shut with a slam.

"Phoebe," Troy says as we walk back to his room, his voice low and serious, "if Urian hasn't figured out who sent the e-mail in time, I *will* go to the courtyard with you." Before I can argue, he adds, "You're my friend and I couldn't stand it if you got hurt."

My argument dies on my tongue. It's hard to be mad at concern like that. But that doesn't change what I have to do.

"If the computer genius hasn't figured it out," I say, "you can walk me to the courtyard. But I'm going in alone." When he starts to argue, I say, "I appreciate that you're worried about me, but I won't let anything jeopardize finding out the truth about my dad."

I can tell he still wants to argue, but I can also tell that he gets how important this is to me. He nods. Reluctantly.

I just hope I'm not doing something stupid. Again.

When Nic and I walk out of the boys' dorm, the sun is riding low in the sky. I check my watch. It's six o'clock. If I'm quick, I can run home and grab some dinner before I have to meet Griffin at the dock.

As I step off the front stairs, about to say good-bye to Nicole, movement to my left catches my eyes.

Griffin.

I smile automatically and am about to call out to him when I realize something very important. It's Griffin. Going into the girls' dorm. And Adara is standing on the front step to greet him.

Suddenly I'm not so hungry anymore.

chapter 8

AUTOPORTATION

SOURCE: ZEUS

The ability to move oneself to a different location through nonphysical means. Maximum distance traveled depends on strength and skill of powers. Autoportation to a previously unvisited place is prohibited because of the inherent risk of arriving in an undesirable, perilous, or public location.

DYNAMOTHEOS STUDY GUIDE © Stella Petrolas

WHEN THE LAST RAY of sunlight disappears, I'm planted on the couch reading last month's *Runner's World*. Well, I'm *pretending* to read last month's *Runner's World*. My eyes are skimming across the pages and everything, but my mind hasn't taken in a single word. It's too busy screaming, *Griffin is back together with Adara!*

Through some major act of willpower—or hopelessness—my eyes aren't even full of tears.

I hear giggling seconds before the front door opens. "You are so right," Stella says, looking over her shoulder as she walks in. "I'll have to add that to my résumé."

I don't feel like facing Stella right now. Wishing I'd retreated to my room earlier, I bury my face in my magazine, hoping I can blend

in with the unfortunately white couch. Why did the MY SPORT IS
YOUR SPORT'S PUNISHMENT tee have to be cherry red?

"Phoebe," a rebel-boy voice says in greeting.

I peek over the top of an article about avoiding knee injuries.
The recipient of Stella's giggling is none other than Xander. Great.
All I need is him taunting me at home, too.

"I didn't know you were home," Stella says, looking like a kid
caught sneaking an extra cookie. Yeah, a Xander-shaped cookie.
Her two-shades-darker-than-her-hair eyebrows draw into a frown. "I
thought you were meeting—"

"I'm not," I interrupt. She knows exactly where I was supposed to
be right now. I don't need the reminder. I don't even want to hear
his name.

She looks surprised, but doesn't comment. Smart girl. In my
present mood, I'm itching to test my current powers control. She
would make the perfect guinea pig. In fact—

"Xander and I were just talking about you actually," she says, giving him a warm smile and distracting me before I actually try to
turn her into a rodent. She is blissfully unaware of how close she
came to becoming someone's pet. "Discussing that exercise I was
telling you about earlier."

I glance at the object of her adoration. He's standing just inside
the door, like he'd rather keep out of the line of fire, with his hands
tucked into the back pockets of his jeans. Watching me with those
unusual lavender eyes, he doesn't move a muscle. Like a statue. His
face remains unreadable.

Typical guy. Keeps everything hidden so you have to guess what he's thinking. So a girl's imagination can run rampant until confronted with incontrovertible proof of her suspicions.

"Good for you." I snap my magazine shut and get up from the couch. If they're going to be here, giggling and talking about me, I'm locking myself in my room. Figuratively, of course, since my door doesn't lock.

"Actually"—she glances at Xander—"we could try that exercise with the glass of water—"

"Not," I say, my pent-up emotion barely contained, "tonight."

I can practically hear her mouth drop.

She'll get over it. Or not. Either way, playing counselor and camper is not on my agenda for the night. The last thing I want is to be around people. Solitude and the comfort of my bed are calling. That, and a box of tissues.

I'm almost to my room when I feel a hand clamp over my shoulder.

"Running away isn't going to help," Xander says.

"I'm not running away from anything." I spin around, shrugging off his hand. "I'm going to my room for some privacy, thank you very much."

He crosses his arms over his chest and cocks his brows, like he dares me to lie again. "Denying your feelings can affect your powers."

"Oh yeah?" I snap brilliantly. "You don't know anything about my feelings. Or my situation."

"I know more than you think." He steps closer, his voice barely a growl. "You mentioned my expulsion earlier. Do you know *why* I was expelled?"

I shake my head.

"Because three years ago," he whispers, "*I* had to take the test." His mouth is right next to my ear when he adds, "And I *didn't* pass."

My heart thwacks against my chest. *Xander* is the other student who had to take the test. *Xander* failed the test. *Xander* got expelled for a year.

"What did you—" I shake my head and start over. "What happened when you failed?"

He leans back, his lavender eyes completely blank.

"I hope you never find out," he says. Then he turns and stalks through the kitchen and out the back door.

Stella stares at the door for several seconds, before turning on me. "What did you—"

"You couldn't have told me earlier?" I snap.

Her cheeks flush and I think, for the first time since we met, she's actually embarrassed about something. Good.

"You lied," I accuse. "About your student passing the test."

"I didn't," she insists. "I was Xander's tutor *after* he failed. I helped him pass on his second attempt."

"Whatever."

I spin and head for my room.

The roller coaster is finally getting to me. Thankfully, I make it to the safety of my room and collapse on my bed before the tears start. I think I'm going through what therapist Mom would call an

157

emotional release. More like an emotional flood. Between the looming test and my dad's missing record and Griffin, it's amazing my emotions are holding together at all. I wouldn't be surprised if they just gave up on me altogether and—

Knock, knock.

Over the pounding beat of my heart, I wipe at my tears and say, "I'm not here."

Whoever it is doesn't wait for a response.

"Phoebe?" Griffin asks. "I thought we were meeting at seven."

His voice sounds perfectly normal.

Of course it does. He doesn't know what I know—what I saw, what I felt. Why should he even suspect that I know he's back with his ex-girlfriend? He must think he's kept it a pretty tight secret.

I squeeze my eyes together for a second, willing—begging—my unshed tears to disappear. They are a weakness I can't afford.

"Yeah, well," I say, pushing up to my feet while keeping my back to him, buying myself a few more seconds. "You thought wrong."

"What's the matter?" He comes up behind me and puts his hands on my shoulders, trying to turn me around. He has the nerve to sound concerned. "What happened?"

I stiffen against his touch. "Nothing."

"Are you crying?" When I shake my head, not trusting myself to speak again, he says, "You *are* crying."

Despite my best efforts, he half turns me around and half slides around so we're face-to-face. I close my eyes. I just can't look at him right now. Not when all I see is him talking to Adara, going into the bookstore with Adara, meeting Adara at her dorm. It's too much.

"Talk to me," he demands.

I feel his fingers on my cheeks, wiping my sad excuse for tears away. Which only makes them fall harder.

His forehead touches mine and he whispers, "Please."

I take several long, deep breaths.

"Where were you this afternoon?" I finally ask.

He hesitates for a split second. "I told you, I—"

My eyes fly open. "Do. *Not*. Lie to me."

I step back, needing space to think clearly.

I can see him thinking. Beneath his dark curls, his bright blue eyes don't budge from mine; he doesn't blink. Then, after several long seconds, he closes his eyes, sucks in a deep breath, and says, "Aunt Lili and I got back and done with the stocking early. I was visiting a friend in the dorms."

"Adara."

He hesitates, then says, "Yes."

"What?" I'm shocked he admitted the truth.

"Yes." He looks like he is afraid to say more. "Yes, I was visiting Dara."

"Why have you been lying to me?" I can hear the icy edge in my voice and I don't like it. I don't like how he's making me feel right now. Jealous. With a neon capital *J*. "You've been spending all your time with her. Like yesterday. At the bookstore."

He doesn't show any signs of shock that I didn't buy his story about looking for a training book.

"You're right," he says, and my heart tries to pound out of my chest. "I met Adara at the bookstore yesterday."

And lied about it.

"But it's not what you think."

"Then tell me what it *is*," I demand.

Gods, I hate how I sound like such a jealous girlfriend, but it's not like he's not giving me a reason to distrust. I close my eyes and suddenly I'm reliving the last time I felt like this. Junior prom. More than a year ago now, but I remember like it was yesterday.

I had known something was wrong when Justin didn't show to pick me up. A smarter girl might have taken that as a sign, but I believed in him. Trusted him. Something must have come up. Rather than curl up with a box of tissues and a cup of self-pity, I called Cesca and got a ride with her and her date. When I climbed into the limo and saw the look of pure sympathy in her eyes, that's when I knew.

By the time we pulled up at the glamorous Sunset Tower Hotel, I was ready for the confrontation. I stormed into the dance, scanned the room until I found Justin at a table in the far corner, and marched right up to him.

"Where were you?" I demanded.

"Let's not do this here, Phoebe," Justin had said. "Why don't we go out to my car and—"

"No," I shouted, hands fisted on my hips, on the silver satin of the bustier dress that had taken me weeks to find. The perfect dress. "I deserve to know."

He'd hesitated, deciding whether to lie.

Just like Griffin did tonight.

Only tonight feels infinitely worse. Because I love Griffin infinitely more.

That realization clenches around my heart.

"I—" He jams his fingers through his curls. "Phoebe, I can't tell you."

Everything inside me stills.

At least Justin had the decency to confess dumping me for Mitzi Busch because her knees weren't Super Glued shut like mine. Griffin wasn't even pretending to admit the truth.

"Then I don't believe you." My heart splinters a little with every word.

"I can't make you believe me," he says, dropping his hands and taking a step back. "I thought we were past the distrusting stage. I thought you knew me better than this. Better than anyone."

I can't look away from his blue eyes, a little less bright thanks to the betrayal I see there. But the truth is, he lied to me. More than once. And now, even though he's admitted to lying to me, he won't tell me the whole truth. He's not the only one who feels betrayed.

"So did I," I say, turning away and walking to my desk.

"Phoebe, I didn't mean to—"

"I'd like you to leave." My voice cracks as I add, "Now."

I stand in front of my desk, afraid to move until he does—afraid that my heart will shatter completely. For a long time there's just silence, stillness in the air, as I can feel him watching me.

"I'm not Justin," he whispers.

Then, all of a sudden, it's like a vacuum sucks all the air out of my room. The next thing I hear is the click of my door closing behind him as he leaves.

I collapse into my desk chair, folding my arms over my laptop and laying my cheek on the smooth, plastic surface. My heart feels like it's been ripped out of my chest. The oracle was wrong. Griffin and I aren't fated for anything more than heartache.

It's not until I feel the wetness on my arm that I realize I'm crying on my laptop. The last thing I need is to fry my connection to the outside world. I sit up, wipe away my tears, and lift the top on my laptop. I've never needed Nola and Cesca more in my life, and if one of them isn't online, I don't know what I'll do.

But when I log in to chat, I see blank little faces next to their screen names.

Right. Cesca's probably in Paris by now. Nola's probably at the library doing research for her study. How can they both have so much great stuff going on when my life is a mess?

Yeah, I know that's totally self-centered. It's not fair for me to begrudge them good stuff. Especially since we're best friends.

Not one person on my friends list is online. Not Cesca or Nola, not Nicole, not Troy. Not even the gorgon cheerleader queen—trust me, if I could get Adara off my friends list I would, but the Academy IM system seems to have a twisted sense of humor about this. How can everyone be unavailable when I need them?

While I'm staring at the screen through tear-fogged eyes, a yellow smiley face shows up next to Nola's screen name.

Thank the gods!

I open up a new chat window.

LostPhoebe: Nola!

GranolaGrrl: hey Phoebes

GranolaGrrl: what's up?

LostPhoebe: I think Griffin and I just broke up

GranolaGrrl: omigods what happened??

I bite my lip to keep from crying. More.

LostPhoebe: he's cheating on me

GranolaGrrl: of course he's not!

LostPhoebe: he is

LostPhoebe: with Adara

GranolaGrrl: his ex? that's nuts

GranolaGrrl: he's crazy about you

LostPhoebe: he's been spending lots of time with her

GranolaGrrl: maybe there's a reasonable explanation

Nola always sees the good in people. While this is a great trait in a best friend—she always looks past my bad attitude when I'm in a crappy mood—she's not the most discerning when it comes to character. She blindly believes the best until presented with incontrovertible proof. Sometimes not even then.

LostPhoebe: there's more

LostPhoebe: he was in her dorm room this afternoon

LostPhoebe: when he told me he was helping his aunt

GranolaGrrl: are you sure?

GranolaGrrl: did you ask him about it?

LostPhoebe: he admitted it

LostPhoebe: he says it's not what I think

LostPhoebe: but he won't tell me what it *is*

GranolaGrrl: I'm so sorry sweetie

New tears rush to my eyes. If even Nola is willing to accept that I'm right, then all my niggling doubts are gone. How could I have been so stupid over a guy . . . again?

GranolaGrrl: I know how much he means to you

LostPhoebe: guess it wasn't mutual

GranolaGrrl: you never know

GranolaGrrl: he might still surprise you

LostPhoebe: doubt it

GranolaGrrl: promise me you'll give him a chance to explain

LostPhoebe: I did

LostPhoebe: he wouldn't

GranolaGrrl: give him one more chance

GranolaGrrl: for me

I almost say I won't. I don't want to. But for Nola, only for Nola, I will.

LostPhoebe: okay

LostPhoebe: for you

GranolaGrrl: I need to go

GranolaGrrl: you okay?

LostPhoebe: I'll be fine

GranolaGrrl: I'll be online again later

GranolaGrrl: love you

LostPhoebe: love you too

LostPhoebe: thanks

I stare at the chat screen until her smiley face disappears.

Instead of feeling better, reassured, I feel a little more empty after chatting with Nola. She didn't exactly say what I wanted to hear. That's Nola, though. She always says and does what's right, not what's convenient or comforting.

Almost automatically, needing something to keep my mind busy, I click on the icon to check my e-mail. Three new messages. One from Adara—no thank you. I click on the message and am about to drag it to the trash when I see the folder I made when I was mad at Griffin last year. "Liars." I drop her e-mail in there. Even if she hasn't lied to me, I bet she would if I gave her the chance.

The second e-mail is from Mrs. Philipoulos.

To: Library Employees

Cc: headmaster@theacademy.gr

Bcc: lostphoebe@theacademy.gr

From: librarylady@theacademy.gr

Subject: Secret Archives Access

Former Academy library employees,

Upon a recent inspection of the library secret archives, I have discovered two missing volumes in the Mount Olympus records. If you have any knowledge of the theft or whereabouts for these volumes, please contact me immediately. No punitive action will be taken if the volumes are returned within the week.

Also, please remember that your right to access the secret archives depends on your status as a library employee. If you are no longer working in the library, you should not access the secret archives for ANY reason.

Yours,

Philippa Philipoulos

At least she only blind-copied me. Damian won't know I'm involved. I wouldn't want him to get suspicious and rush home from his honeymoon. The last thing I need is Mom and Damian nosing around in the middle of my trying to find out what happened to Dad.

Mrs. Philipoulos said two volumes are missing. Clearly, one of them is Dad's trial record. I wonder what else was taken.

The last e-mail is yet another blocked message.

To: lostphoebe@theacademy.gr

From: [Blocked]

Subject: [No Subject]

Urian Nacus will not be able to decrypt my identity before our meeting.

Do not be late.

Just for ducks, I click print. When the blank page spits out, I slide it back into the paper tray. I'm so not surprised. If e-mails one and two wouldn't print, it would be some kind of divine intervention if the third did.

Closing down my computer, I decide I need to get out of my room, out of this house. I need the clarity of thought that only running can bring. I grab the zip-up sweatshirt off the back of my chair. As I hurry through the living room, I try not to make eye contact. Xander is back and I'm not up for conversation. I can see him and Stella sitting on the couch—Stella flirtatiously turned to face him with one foot tucked up underneath her and Xander nonflirtatiously focused on whatever he's writing in a spiral notebook.

Maybe I can get to the front door—

"Phoebe," Stella calls out before I can escape, "are you okay?"

"Fine," I say, hoping she'll take the hint.

Of course subtlety is not her strong suit.

"Griffin looked pretty upset when he left." She climbs off the couch and approaches me. Dropping her voice to a whisper, she asks, "Is everything all right?"

"Just peachy," I say, and I can't quite keep the emotion out of my voice.

But instead of pouncing on my trauma—I can just see her gloating to Adara over my continued torment—she puts her hand on my shoulder and says, "I'm sorry." And then shocks the Hades out of me by adding, "If you ever need someone to talk to . . ."

"Sure." I try to smile—and hide my shock at her apparently sincere offer. "Thanks."

She smiles sympathetically.

"I'm going for a run," I say, uncomfortable with this friendly Stella. I jerk my hand back over my shoulder, "I need some fresh air."

Xander looks up at me, his lavender eyes wide and intent. He looks like he might say something, but I turn and head outside before he gets the chance.

I take the front steps two at a time. Those same steps where Griffin almost first kissed me. Right after I found out he was a dutybound descendant of Hercules. Right before I found out I was part of some elaborate bet between him and Stella and Adara. I should have listened to my gut the first time. Then my heart wouldn't be shattering right now.

Maybe I shouldn't be surprised at our rocky end. We had a pretty rocky beginning, even if the time between was smooth and wonderful.

"Phoebe," Xander calls out. Then, when I don't stop, he shouts, "Castro!"

I. Have. Had. Enough.

Whipping around and jogging back to the porch, I snap, "What?"

"I'm sorry," he says—like he knows an apology is the only thing that can undermine my fury. "I shouldn't have stormed out like that earlier. You're going through a tough enough time without my making things worse."

"Fine," I say. "Apology accepted. Can I go now?"

Before he can answer, I turn and jog down the path leading to the dock—to the beach. To my left, the front lawn of the Academy stretches out into a rolling green hill that leads down to the cove. Ahead, I can see the Aegean, inky black and rippling in reflected moonlight from the starry sky. It's so peaceful and calming and completely at odds with the emotions running through me.

How can Griffin make me feel so good and so rotten at the same time? Why did he go back to Adara? Does she have something I don't—other than bleached blonde hair and a cheerleader uniform?

Does she, like Mitzi Busch, *offer* something I haven't?

When he said he didn't know why he'd stayed with her so long, I'd believed him. When he told me about his mom's oracle reading, I'd really thought we'd be together forever. I'd thought he was my *one*.

Had I really been such a fool?

With only a hint of a moon out tonight, I can barely see the path down to the dock. It's only because I've climbed this path dozens of times that I make it to the bottom without stumbling. Usually I take a right, to the long stretch of perfect white beach that just screams for a run. But tonight the tide is really low and there's a thin sliver of shore leading off to the left.

Without another thought, I head left. The strip of sand—still wet from a higher tide and solid beneath my Nikes—winds beneath the cliffs and the village perched overhead. It's quiet and secluded—the beach isn't usually bustling with activity after dark unless it's bonfire night—and it's a relief to know I won't be running into anyone. Company is the last thing I'm looking for. As I hurdle a low rock outcropping, I think about my promise to Nola. She always gives people second chances. And third and fourth and fifth chances. So it's not exactly a surprise that she wants me to give Griff a second opportunity to explain. I don't want to—I feel like I've already given him tons of opportunities—but I can't break a promise. Not to Nola.

I'm just wondering how to go about giving Griffin another chance to explain—do I go after him, or do I wait until he comes to me?—when I feel water slosh over my Nikes.

"What the—?"

I look down. The sliver of beach is two feet thinner than when I started out. I hope it just naturally narrows down as it goes. But a quick glance behind me reveals that the entire strip of beach is disappearing. About a hundred yards back, it's completely gone. Which can only mean one thing.

"Rising tides," I exclaim.

How could I have been so stupid? If the tide is low and I'm suddenly seeing a beach that's never been there before, it's probably because it's not there during high tide. "Stupid, stupid, stupid."

I have to decide quickly what to do, because it's not like I can scale the cliffs if the tide comes in. Behind me, the beach is already underwater. My only choice is to press on and hope the beach opens up around the curve up ahead.

Kicking into a sprint, I try to calm my racing heart. Fear sends adrenaline pumping through my blood, and that's only going to cloud my judgment.

I've never been a short-distance dasher, but I make the two hundred yards to the curve in the beach in record time.

My calves are on fire and my heart is racing out of control. I've never felt so keyed up.

As I speed around the rocks, I heave a huge gasp of relief. There's a nice wide beach, deep enough to stick around for high tide. Some of it even looks familiar.

There's a cluster of bushes along the cliff wall that I know I've seen before. I remember—it's the beach where Griffin took me when we made up last fall. The last training session before the Cycladian Cup.

That's when I know that one day I'll thank Nola for making me give Griffin a second chance. The memory of how great it felt to know he cared about me, how great it felt to take his hand and know that nothing stood between us anymore. I want that again.

"What do you mean you didn't tell her?" a muffled female voice demands.

I'm not sure what makes me do it—instinct, fear, or knowledge beyond my years—but I dive behind a big boulder. I hear the sound of footsteps on gravel and then silence. Whoever was talking must have just reached the beach.

"How could I?" an intimately familiar male voice replies.

Griffin.

"She still doesn't trust me," he says. "She thinks I'm cheating on her."

"Oh, and *not* telling her what's going on is definitely going to make that better."

Is that Adara? I can't see for sure. I dare a peek around the edge of the boulder and catch a glimpse of blonde. Her back is to me, so I can't tell. But it has to be . . . right?

"I know that, Nicole," he says.

Nicole?

Everything crashes to a stop. There's no wind whistling through the trees. No waves crashing on the beach. No breath leaving my body.

"You can't tell Phoebe," he says. "If she knew what was going on, then she might . . ."

The rest of his sentence gets lost as the world rushes back to life around me. There's a roaring in my ears that I can't shake away. Then my hearing finally clears as he says, "I don't want her to get hurt."

Why does Nicole know the secret I'm not allowed to know? And why would whatever they're doing wind up hurting me? It's bad enough knowing Griffin has betrayed me with Adara. I expect that from her and should have known better about him. But Nicole? She is the closest thing I have to a best friend on this island.

How could they do this to me?

In that instant, my mind focuses entirely on one thing: getting away from this beach. Away from where I learned about this latest betrayal. Away, away, away.

Eyes closed, I feel a tingling spread over my skin.

When I blink open, I'm in my room.

Great, I finally do something useful with my powers, and I can't even enjoy it. I'm too busy worrying about my world crumbling around me.

* * * * *

"I didn't hear you come home," Stella says when I stumble out of my room two tear-filled hours later.

I barely glance at her before continuing to the kitchen. All my crying has left me severely dehydrated and I need liquid like nobody's business. Taking a dirty glass from the sink, I fill it with tap water and chug. I don't even have the energy to twist the cap off a Gatorade.

"What happened to you?"

I flick Stella a glance over my glass. Her generally superior look gradually fades as I just stare at her.

When I finish the last drop in my glass, I set it in the sink and start to leave the kitchen. Stella steps in front of me. She grabs my shoulders with both hands, dips down to look in my eyes, and announces, "You *autoported*."

"What?"

"*Autoported*," she repeats. "You shimmered yourself home, didn't you?"

"How can you tell?" Then I remember she can read minds. "Never mind."

"No," she says, shaking her head. "Your mind's too much of a mess for me to read right now. You have a residual glow in your eyes. That only happens when someone has recently *autoported*."

I shrug. I'm in no mood to be analyzed or critiqued or judged or whatever she's trying to do right now.

"I know you're hurting," she says, her voice soft with understanding, "but *autoportation* is the most advanced of all *dynamotheos* powers. We need to figure out how this happened."

"Stella, I—"

She squeezes my shoulders. "I wouldn't ask you to do this right now unless I thought it was really important."

Her pale gray eyes are steely with resolve. Clearly, I'm not escaping this session. "Just let me splash some water on my face."

Stella nods and lets me go freshen up.

When I get back, she's in the dining room with a bunch of papers spread out over the table. She glances up when I walk in.

"Feeling better?"

"A little," I answer honestly.

"Good," she says, "because I need you to tell me everything about the situation that led to your *autoportation*."

As I sink into the chair opposite hers, I meet her eyes straight on. I don't really want to tell her what just happened—we may be friendly at the moment, but that doesn't mean I'm about to share personal details of my love life. But, the truth is, I'm a little freaked out by the whole *autoportation* thing. It's not like I controlled it. I didn't even see it coming.

What if I accidentally *autoport* myself to the Gobi Desert? Or the bottom of the ocean? Or the middle of a Mary-Kay convention? I shudder at the thought of all the makeup and pep.

Considering the risks of *not* understanding what happened, it's far less frightening to tell Stella the truth.

"Well, I went for a run," I begin. "To clear my head . . ."

For the next thirty minutes, I spill every last detail of the last few days, everything from the instant I turned Damian into a surfer dude up until I *autoported* back to my room. I even trash on Adara and her boyfriend-stealing games, despite the fact that she and Stella are friends.

Stella doesn't say a word. Just scribbles notes in a pink spiral-bound while I babble on. And on. And on.

"All I could think of was being away from there and then ..." I gesture toward my room. "I was."

Finished, I take a deep breath and slump back against my chair. Wow. I feel a lot better just getting that off my chest.

"I'd like to try an experiment," Stella finally says. She places her pen in the center of the table. "Simple *telekinesis*. Pick this up."

When I start to reach for it, she says, "No. Not with your hands."

Okay. Concentrating all my energy on the pen, I try to move it toward me. Instead of sliding in my direction, though, it spins in circles for several seconds before flying off the table and heading point first into the nearest wall.

"I know what your problem is," she announces.

"Great." I'm glad someone does. "Tell me."

"You were trying to *move* the pen."

"Well, duh." I hold her gaze to keep from rolling my eyes—she is trying to help me, after all. "That's what you told me to do."

"The approach is all wrong." She pushes back from the table and retrieves the pen from the wall. "You were thinking about moving the pen—which you did—when you need to think about having the pen in your hand."

I shake my head. "I don't get it."

Stella replaces the pen on the table. "Focus your thoughts on the pen being in your hand already. Imagine it there. Believe it is already in your—"

While she is talking, I try what she suggests. I picture the pen in my hand, like I can already feel the cool plastic in my palm. And then, while Stella is still talking and I'm still skeptically expecting the pen to zip into the living room, I feel a gentle weight in my hand.

When I glance down, Stella's pen is lying across my palm.

"I did it," I say, stunned. Looking up at her, I repeat, "Omigods, I did it!"

She takes her pen back and starts scribbling more notes.

"Does that mean I'm cured?"

Glancing up, gray eyes sparkling, she says, "Not yet." Before I can slump in defeat, she adds, "But it's a start."

We share a smile of success. For the first time in my life, a success off the cross-country course feels almost as good as winning a race. Almost. But, like Stella said, it's a start.

chapter 9

TELEKINESIS

SOURCE: ARES

The ability to move objects through nonphysical means. Ability varies depending on size and weight of object and distance moved. May be combined with Aerokinesis to magnify strength of ability. Generally the first power to manifest in young hematheos.

DYNAMOTHEOS STUDY GUIDE © Stella Petrolas

MONDAY MORNING I show up on the Academy steps early. Not that I'm eager for camp or anything, but after spending all last night—and the three previous nights—trying to get to sleep, I just couldn't stare at my ceiling a minute longer. At first I thought the Internet could be my diversion. But I finally disconnected Saturday afternoon after another unprintable blocked message and after moving the fifth e-mail from Griffin, unread, into the "Liars" folder. Even running myself to the point of exhaustion three days in a row hadn't helped.

At least camp will be a welcome distraction.

"Never thought I'd see you here early."

I turn at the sound of Xander's voice.

"Yeah, I could say the same about you," I say, leaning my head back against the cold marble column.

I hear his footsteps approach and then the sounds of him sitting next to me, but don't open my eyes. With exactly zero hours of sleep and coming down from a weekend-long emotional roller coaster, I'm not in the mood.

Apparently, though, he's not sensing my go-away vibes.

"Trouble in paradise?" he asks. Despite the cliché, he sounds serious.

"What do you care?"

"I don't."

I feel him lean back next to me against the column.

"Good," I say.

For a minute I think he's not going to say anything else. "Unless it's affecting your powers training."

Prying an eye open, I ask, "I beg your pardon?"

"If your problems with Blake are going to get in the way of your development, then we need to deal with this."

"My problems with Blake—" I shake my head, "with *Griffin* have nothing to do with my powers."

"You don't think so?" He sounds all superior. Maybe he and Stella have more in common than I thought. "Let me tell you from experience that *everything* that affects your emotions affects your powers."

Right. I almost forgot about his *experience*.

My spine stiffens as I turn my full attention on him. "Which reminds me," I snap. "You could explain a little more about the test—and the consequences of *failing it*—since you've, you know, *done that*."

His lavender eyes burn brighter for a second, but he doesn't betray any other reaction.

"My experience has nothing to do with yours," he says, his voice sincere. "The gods play their games as they see fit, and what happened to me is completely removed from whatever will happen to you. It is intensely personal."

"It could still be useful," I insist, "if I had some hint of what to expect."

I mean, seriously. The solstice is just days away. And even though I earned a handful of merit badges last week—mostly by accident—I feel completely unprepared. My minor success with Stella's pen isn't exactly a guarantee of success. After Xander's cryptic I-hope-you-never-find-out-about-the-consequences comment, getting smoted for accidental powers usage is losing ground on the fear scale in the face of suffering some unknown punishment for failing the test.

"Fine," he says with a sigh. "But it won't help you."

"We'll see."

"It was an unimportant Thursday in Level 10." His eyes get a faraway look, and it's like he's not here anymore. "The girl I'd been dating for three years walked up to me in the cafeteria and, in front of the entire school, announced she was dumping me for some descendant of Zeus because he was better-looking."

I blink at him a few times. When he doesn't continue, I say, "And . . ."

"And thirty seconds later, she and the new guy were deep in the heart of King Minos' labyrinth."

That seems like a bit of an overreaction.

"As I said, the test is intensely personal." He rubs a hand over his face, like he's suddenly very tired. "For anyone else, that wouldn't have been a big deal. For me . . . well, let's just say my family history makes me kind of sensitive about superficial stuff."

"Oh-kay . . ."

"My emotions got the better of me that day," he says. "And I spent the next ten months paying for the lapse. Without Stella's help, I'd probably still be there. If Blake is messing with your emotions, we need to take care of it."

There is something ominous in his tone.

"I don't need your—or anybody else's—help when it comes to Griffin."

"I'm not trying to provoke you, Phoebe," he says, leveling his hypnotic lavender gaze on me. "Just keep in mind that sometimes when you tell yourself things are fine, you're really just driving the tough stuff even deeper."

"Good morning, Xander," Stella's extra-cheerful voice calls out, breaking the spell of his mesmerizing eyes. As she reaches our spot at the base of the column, she looks at me. "Phoebe."

"Stella," Xander says as he climbs to his feet. After a quick nod, he strides off through the Academy's golden doors.

She watches him walk away with a sad, puppy-dog look in her eyes.

I must be feeling generous or something, because I say, "You should ask him out already."

"What do you mean?" Startled, she looks at me. "What makes you think I'm interested in Xander?"

"Puh-lease," I say, pushing up from the cold marble. "Don't play innocent with me. I learned your tricks months ago."

She purses out her lips, like she wants to refute my claim. Then her gray eyes flick to the door Xander just walked through and her whole face softens.

"Do you—" Stella has never looked this vulnerable before. "Do you really think he might . . ."

"You never know until you try."

For several long seconds she watches me, evaluating me. Then she turns on her heel and hurries after him.

As soon as she's gone, I'm thinking about what Xander said. And wondering if he's right. Either way, I need to sort out my feelings.

What if I am just making assumptions about Griffin? What if I'm making a big huge deal out of what he's doing with Adara, when there's really a totally innocent explanation? But if there were, he would have told me. When he told me there was nothing romantic going on between him and Adara, he would have told me what *was* going on. Wouldn't he?

An image of Cesca flashes in my mind. A memory of last year, when I had a secret of my own that I couldn't tell my best friends.

What if it's something like that?

My head is going to spin off my neck if I keep going in circles like this.

"Hi, Phoebe!" Tansy bounds up the steps.

"Hey, Tansy," I reply, still a little distracted by my thoughts, but relieved to have someone nonconfusing to talk to. "What's up?"

"Ready for camp," she says. "Actually, I wanted to ask you a question."

Shaking off my thoughts of secrets, I say, "Shoot."

"How do you become a runner?"

I look at her and smile. "I don't think a person *becomes* a runner," I say. "You either run or you don't."

She bites her lower lip, like she's worried about what to say next.

"Do you run?" I ask.

Green eyes wide, she looks up at me and nods. Even though she's only twelve—not fully developed physically or anything—I can tell she's got the body of a runner. Long proportions, a little gawky. If she's got the drive, she could be an excellent runner.

I smile big. "Then you're a runner."

As soon as I say that, she positively beams. "I want to be just like you."

"No you don't," I reply. No one wants to be like me. Not on this island, anyway. At first it was because I wasn't one of them. Now it's because I am, but I'm still different. Higher up on the family tree. Closer to Olympus. Life was so much easier when I was nothing more exciting than a distance runner. "I'm not that great."

"I think you are."

Her voice is quiet and serious, like she just said the most important thing ever.

I study her, looking at me with a little hero worship in her eyes. It's been so long since someone—anyone—looked up to me that I almost don't know how to react. Back at Pacific Park, I'd been kind of a mentor to a couple of the younger girls on the team. They looked to me for advice and encouragement. That feels like a lifetime ago.

As I look into Tansy's serious eyes, my long-lost big sister instinct kicks in.

"I'm kinda looking for a training partner," I say as we head into the building. "You interested?"

"Really?" she says, her voice full of awe.

Since the position of my current training partner seems to be in question, then yeah, I wouldn't mind having someone else to run with. She might keep my mind off all the times Griffin and I ran together.

"Yeah," I say, trying to play it cool so she doesn't think I'm desperate. "I'm training for the Pythian Games trials and could use a buddy."

We head through the halls of the Academy, toward the courtyard, with her staring wide-eyed and mouth gaping. It's a miracle she doesn't walk into a trash can.

"Is that a yes?"

"Omigods, yes!" she squeals. "When do we start?"

"I've been training in the morning." I push through the door leading to the courtyard. "Why don't you meet me at eight tomorrow on the cross-country course."

Tansy gasps. "Great!"

"Welcome, campers," Adara calls across the courtyard. She spears me with a vicious glance. "We'll be partnering for today's first exercise. Phoebe, you'll be pairing up with me."

Yeah, great.

⁂

"You're not even trying."

I glare at Adara. "Of course I'm trying."

I'm just not succeeding.

"I know how hard it is for you to accept that other people might know something more than you," she snaps, and if I could see her face I know she'd be sneering. "But believe me when I tell you, you're *not* trying."

We've been standing back-to-back for the last half hour, with me trying to materialize a hazelnut latte into her hands. So far I've come up with a coconut, a jar of peanut butter, and—on my most successful attempt—a glass of milk.

I've trained my whole life. Physical training—running, weight lifting, nutritional planning—that's all second nature to me. But this mental training is totally different. I'm not used to consciously exercising my mind and my emotions. Is it any wonder this isn't going well?

"Maybe if you weren't badgering me the whole time," I snap back, pushing away from her and turning around, "I would be able to concentrate."

She spins around, her vapid blue eyes narrowing.

"I don't think this has anything to do with your concentration."

"Oh yeah," I say brilliantly. "What *does* it have to do with, then, your genuisness?"

Instead of answering, she crooks her finger at me before turning and stalking out of the courtyard. Like I'm going to follow *her* anywhere.

I cross my arms over my chest and stand my ground.

Suddenly, she shimmers—*autoports*—into place right in front of my nose.

"I have never been more mad at anyone in my life than I am at you right now," she grinds out through clenched teeth. "Unless you want to spend the next three days on holiday in the underworld, I suggest you join me in the hall. Now."

Then, just as quickly as she appeared, she disappears again.

I look helplessly around the courtyard, but all the ten-year-olds are focusing on the exercise, with Stella, Xander, and Miss Orivas closely supervising.

Okay, if Adara wants to have it out, I'll have it out.

Stomping after her, I'm about ready to unleash my tirade when I catch sight of her eyes. They're all red. And full of tears.

That stops me in my tracks.

If she's so mad at me, why is she crying?

"No," she interrupts before I can say anything. "You listen to me, Phoebe Castro. We both know you're not my favorite person on this island, but I'm going to put that aside for the sake of someone I care about very much." She takes a deep breath, like she's composing herself, before saying, "What you are doing to Griffin is awful."

"What I'm doing to him?" I shake my head. "I'm not doing anything—"

"You're breaking his heart."

I freeze, midsentence. My mouth drops open. It's not just what she said, but how her voice cracks as she says it. Had anyone asked me fifteen seconds ago, I would have sworn up and down on a stack of gold medals that Adara Spencer was incapable of actual human emotion.

"You've ignored his e-mails and dodged his phone calls. He tried to catch you at home half a dozen times this weekend. He's been running every beach on this island hoping to find you."

I actually back up a step, shocked by the emotion in her outburst and by what she's telling me.

"I'm only going to say this once," she says quietly. "So listen up. Griffin Blake is head over heels about you. He would never treat you the way you've been treating him." Her voice drops another notch, so low I have to lean in to hear. "He would never doubt you."

"I don't—" I almost say that I don't doubt him, but that's not true. Over the past few days I've proven over and over that I do. Not that my doubts are unfounded. "You're right. I—I don't trust him."

"He doesn't deserve that."

What about me? What do I deserve? Lies and deception?

"Then why won't he tell me what you two have been doing together?"

Adara's gaze is unwavering. "Because I asked him not to."

Doesn't that confirm my doubts?

"Not because there's anything to conceal from you in particular." She tucks her blonde hair behind her ears. "Because I don't want anyone to know what I'm going through."

"What you're—"

"But," she says, glaring at me for interrupting again, "because I care about him so much, I will tell you."

I try not to get hung up on the whole because-I-care-about-him-so-much bit and listen to her explanation. In the few months I've known her, she has never been this serious over anything that doesn't involve nail polish, designer shoes, or a halftime cheer at a wrestling match. An uneasy, my-life-is-about-to-turn-upside-down feeling settles in my stomach.

"My mother is becoming a handmaiden of Apollo."

Er, what?

I know I look totally confused.

"Becoming a handmaiden is an honor and a sacrifice. The chosen must pledge to serve the deity unwaveringly for the duration of her term. That means she is leaving me and my father." Her eyes well up again, and her voice catches. "She will serve on Mount Olympus for the next twenty-five years."

"Wow, that's a long time to work for someone."

"The worst is"—Adara gives me a weak smile—"she can't leave Mount Olympus during her service."

Holy Hades. I shake my head, trying to wrap my brain around that idea. Nic told me that no one—not even *hematheos*—can visit Mount Olympus unless they are in service or on trial. Only an edict from the gods can grant a day pass, and that almost never happens. That means Adara won't see her mom for the next quarter century.

I try to imagine what it would be like not to have Mom to talk to for that long. She'd miss out on my birthdays and my graduations and my—sometime in the distant future—wedding. There would be races, maybe even the Olympics. Every day there are little things that I talk to her about, ask her about. If she weren't around . . . It's unfathomable.

I should e-mail Mom when I get home.

"Adara, I'm so—"

"Sorry?" she asks with a sad laugh. "That's exactly why I didn't want Griffin to tell anyone. I'm not interested in a pity party. Besides, this is supposed to be a prestigious honor for the family. I'm supposed to celebrate"—one hand wipes at a tear streaking down her cheek—"not grieve."

"So, Griffin has been helping you, uh . . ."

"Prepare to lose my mother?" She gives a little snort. "Yeah, pretty much."

I try to wrap my brain around this news. Griffin hasn't been romantically involved with his ex, he's been helping her through a tough time. I can't fault him for that, of course. Besides the whole descendant-of-Hercules obligation thing, deep down he's a sensitive and loyal guy.

I've been so wrapped up in my own issues that I never thought that someone else might be having problems. Adara's life always seemed so perfect. I never once thought she might be going through a tough time.

But why did he lie to *me*? We're supposed to be partners. Equal. He should have known he could tell me the truth in complete confidence. But he couldn't—or wouldn't—confide in me, which means he doesn't trust me. Not completely. That means that, while he's not completely in the right, he does deserve another chance. *We* deserve another chance.

"You gave Griffin a raw deal," she says.

I never thought I'd say this, but she's right. "I did."

"What are you going to do about it?"

"I'll fix it," I vow. As soon as camp is out for the day, I'll be knocking on his door, prepared to work out this whole trust thing.

"You'd better."

When she starts to turn back to the courtyard, I reach out and touch her elbow. "Thank you."

She stiffens. "Whatever," she says, back in old Adara form. "If you're over being pissed at me, maybe we can get on with the *neofaction* exercise."

Less than a minute later, she's standing there with a steaming-hot latte in her hand.

I spin around, ready for my accolades.

She takes a sip and then snorts. "Nice try." The cup glows for a second and then disappears. "That was decaf."

For a second I think about strangling her. But then my common sense kicks in. First of all, I need to focus on controlling my powers if I'm going to pass the test. And second, I don't fancy spending time in Hades.

Sympathy for Adara has nothing to do with my decision to quietly turn around and try again.

Promise.

✦✦✦✦✦

"He didn't mention where he was going," Aunt Lili says when I ask her if Griffin's home.

"Oh," I say, deflated. I want to talk to him as soon as possible. For the first time in a while, I do *not* think the worst. Despite my better judgment—maybe it was her tears or the phase of the moon or a curse of understanding—I believe Adara. "Can you tell him I stopped by. And—" I almost ask her to tell him I'm sorry, but that's definitely the sort of thing a girl needs to say in person. "And that I'll try again tomorrow."

And the day after that. And the day after that. And every day until we're good again. Because what we have is definitely worth the effort—and definitely worth my eating some humble pie.

"My nephew isn't perfect," Aunt Lili says as I reach the door. "But he has a good heart."

"Yeah," I say giving her a confident smile, "I know that." *Now.*

If my trust issues have driven him away, I have no one to blame but myself.

As the door closes behind me, I think about how unfair I was to

Griffin—and to myself—for thinking the worst. After nine months, I should trust him—and my instincts—more than that.

Without thinking, I kick into a jog as I hit the edge of the village. My Nikes pound the smooth stone path with a soft thud. Every step I take sends more blood, more oxygen, pumping through me. My worries start to ooze away. Griffin and I will be fine. If he can't forgive me right away, then I'll work to win him back. We're fated. That's not the kind of thing a girl can let slip away.

I'll pass my test. My control over my powers is getting better every day. Last week I *autoported* and today I materialized—*neofactured*—a dozen lattes for Adara. Even if none of them was to her exacting specifications, she still gave me the merit badge. (This one has an orange ring of color, a yellow background, and a gray factory-building design. I'll line it up on my dresser, next to the other six, when I get home.)

Tomorrow night, I'll meet my mystery e-mailer and find out what happened to Dad. And maybe learn how to keep whatever happened to him from accidentally happening to me.

Running always makes everything so clear.

Maybe this is why I've been so stressed. Most of the running I've done lately is training runs. All business and focus. No time for daydreaming and working through things while physically exhausting myself. Running is definitely my therapy. Starting tomorrow, I'm going to schedule regular fun runs—training-free time.

Before I know it, I'm jogging toward home, following the path that curves around the front lawn of the Academy. But I haven't finished exercising my problems, so I steer off toward campus. A hard run around the cross-country course should do the trick.

Nearly two hours later I'm racing up the front steps at home, exhausted in the best possible way.

Giddy on endorphins, I bust in and shout, "Stella, I'm—"

I stop midsentence.

Lying on the living-room couch, feet propped up on the arm and clearly asleep, is Griffin. He didn't stir when I came shouting into the room. Obviously, he's been out for a while.

"He was on the front porch when I got home from camp," Stella says. She's leaning against the far wall, casually stirring up the fruit in a peach yogurt.

My heart melts big-time.

How could I have been such an idiot? He's made it clear every day in a million different ways how much he cares for me. I was ready to dismiss it all because he was talking to another girl. Because he was helping out a good friend.

I will never be that stupid again. Well, I'll try not to be anyway.

In an instant, I'm sitting on the coffee table at the end by his head.

"I've got some work to do," Stella says, pushing away from the wall. "I'll be in my room. With the door shut. And my headphones on."

I flash her a grateful smile. She's giving us—me—some privacy and I appreciate it. I don't need her to see me begging for forgiveness—she'd never let me live it down.

As soon as she and her yogurt disappear down the hall, I lean forward over Griffin. I take a second to absorb him before I wake him up. I've never seen him sleep before—his thick lashes fan out below his eyes like exotic palm fronds. There is no sign of worry or pain or the weight of his Herculean obligations. Just pure, innocent boy.

My pure, innocent boy.

Hand hovering above his shoulder, I sigh. I don't want to wake him up. I don't want to disturb his peace.

But my sigh must have been a touch too loud or too close—or maybe he just sensed I was there—because his palm-frond lashes flutter open, and instead I'm staring into his bright blue eyes.

For about half a second, his eyes are just as worry-free as his sleeping face had been. He smiles. Then a cloud shadows their brightness.

"Phoebe," he exclaims, lurching up to a sitting position, "I was waiting for you."

I smile nervously. "Clearly."

"I mean, I wanted to talk to you." He looks over my shoulder. "What time is it?"

I check my watch. "Six-thirty."

"*Skata,* I was supposed to meet Dara at six." His eyes pop wide. "I mean—not that I—she doesn't—"

"It's okay," I say, laying a hand on his arm. "She told me."

His eyebrows pinch into a frown and he looks like he's in pain. "I wanted to tell you. You know I did. I just—"

"I know," I say, trying to ease his pain. "You have to help her. It's your Hercules complex."

"No," he says. "It's more than that."

"Then what?" I say, trying to be as open as possible. I won't let there be any more lies and half-truths between us.

"Adara is my friend. Until you helped me work through things with Nicole last year, she was my oldest friend. That's never going to change." He takes my hands and holds them between his, between us. "Neither is the fact that you're my girlfriend."

"I know." I ignore the wetness in my eyes. "I'm sorry I doubted you. I trust you, I really do. But sometimes I just don't trust my own instincts."

"We'll have to work on that," he says, grinning and pulling me off the coffee table and onto his lap.

When he's got me settled, I slip my arms around his neck. "While we're at it, let's work on you trusting me, too."

"Me? I trust you," he insists. "What makes you think I—"

"I saw you with Nicole on the beach the other night." I think back to that night. When I got so upset I'd shimmered myself home. Griffin always said my powers would be affected by my emotions until I learned to master them. "She knew what was going on with Adara."

His brows scrunch over his blue eyes. "You were there?"

I refuse to blush. He doesn't need to know I was hiding behind a boulder. "Why could you tell her the truth and not me?"

His head flops back against the couch. "I didn't tell her," he groans. "She guessed."

"Really?" That's a pretty uncanny guess.

"Interpol could use someone with her instincts. If it makes you feel any better, she was pretty pissed that I hadn't told you." He gives me a half smile. "She let me have it."

194

Score one for Nicole. She always has my back.

"Why did you think the truth would hurt me?" I ask.

"What do you mean?"

"You asked her not to tell me," I explain. "You said you didn't want me to get hurt."

"No, that wasn't about Dara." He turns completely serious. "You know that research project Nic's been working on?"

I nod.

"She's been trying to find a loophole in our parents' punishment decree."

"Wow." I'm breathless. "Can you do that?"

"There have been a few cases." He gives me a sad smile. "But it's very rare."

Rare, but not impossible. My mind floods with possibilities. If there was a way to undo an Olympic decree, then Griffin could get his parents back. Nicole's parents could be un-banished. Dad could get un-smoted.

"Omigods, Griffin," I gasp, overwhelmed with hope. "Do you know what this means? This means we could all—"

"No," he says, cutting me off. "This is why I didn't want to tell you what she's trying to do. This is a one-in-a-billion long shot. The gods are as unyielding as they are fickle, if that makes any sense. They've had millennia to hone their skills at writing unbreakable decrees. The chance that they messed up in one of ours—" He shakes his head. "I don't want to get your hopes up, just to see you get hurt all over again."

His blue eyes are full of the same pain I felt at losing Dad. More, since he lost both his parents at once. But at the same time, deeper than the pain is his love for me. I don't know how I let myself believe that wasn't there.

And because of my love for him, I won't push the issue right now.

"We can talk about this some other time," I say. Relaxing in his arms, I snuggle my head against his neck. "Right now I'm too busy trusting you to think about anything else."

I feel the rumble of his laugh against my chest.

I know he is dead serious about protecting me, about keeping me from pain. I also know that I can't let this go forever. I'm not so dumb that I don't realize what a crazy impossibility this loophole thing is. If there is a chance, though—even the teeny, tiniest, slimmest chance in history—for any of us to get back our lost parents, then I have to pursue that chance.

For now, I'll hang back and let him and Nicole take the lead, helping when I can. But I'll follow this through to the end.

However long it takes.

chapter 10

CORPOPROTECTION

SOURCE: HESTIA

The ability to protect oneself from harm, whether seen or unseen. In some hematheos, *this may manifest as the ability to sense impending danger. Others may be capable of deflecting a direct physical threat. Effectiveness diminished by mental distraction.*

DYNAMOTHEOS STUDY GUIDE © Stella Petrolas

TANSY IS WAITING at the cross-country starting block when Griffin and I walk up the next morning. She's wearing a tank top, supershort running shorts, and a pair of sneakers that look older than me. She's also wearing a headband and matching wristbands in a very eighties white with blue stripes. Oblivious to our approach, she's busy stretching. But not normal stretching—superexaggerated stretching, like a cartoon or something.

"Is that her?" Griffin whispers.

"Uh-huh," I whisper back. With a shrug, I add, "She wants to be a runner."

"She, um . . ." He swallows hard. "Certainly has the outfit down."

"Don't laugh."

"I wouldn't. Besides," he says, "if she starts training with us, she's gonna need those sweatbands."

With a grateful smile, I take his hand and slip my fingers through his.

Tansy finally notices us approaching.

"Hi, Phoebe," she calls out, waving excitedly. "Griffin, right?"

"Yeah," he says, nodding. "I hear you want to be a runner."

Her green eyes flick to me and back to him. With a breathless, dreamy voice, she says, "More than anything."

I remember that kind of desperate wanting. If my dad had asked me the same question eight years ago, I would have replied in exactly the same way. For maybe a little bit of the same reason. More than anything—more than love of the sport or desire to win or the rush of endorphins—I wanted to be close to him. To be like him.

"Let's get started, then," I say, slipping off my hooded sweatshirt and hanging it on the drinking fountain. "Since this is your first training session, I think we should start out easy. Don't want to kill you on your first day." To Griffin, I suggest, "Why don't we take the yellow course."

"Makes sense." He shrugs out of his zip-up sweatshirt and hangs it over mine. "That's the shortest course," he explains to Tansy. "That way if you get worn out, we can stop after one lap."

"I won't get worn out," she insists. "We don't need to do the baby course." She looks personally offended that we would even suggest she couldn't keep up.

I remember feeling like that, like I had something to prove. Like I didn't need people cutting me slack because I could keep up on my own, thank you very much. Just last year I felt like that, actually.

Still, we've never seen her run. To be on the safe side we should at least test the waters before we push her to the limit. That's how injuries happen.

"How about this?" I suggest, going for a middle ground that will save her pride and make sure we don't push her too hard, too fast. "We'll take one lap on the yellow course and then we'll do interval training around the stadium."

"Sounds perfect to me," Griffin says, jogging in place to warm up his muscles. "I read an article about interval training last year. The alternation of sprinting and jogging builds up cardiovascular efficiency and overall stamina faster than running alone."

Tansy looks skeptical, like we're trying to pull one over on her. I am, in a way, but she doesn't necessarily know that.

Finally, after eyeing me and chewing on her lip, she nods. "Okay."

I shake out my arms and legs, checking to make sure they're still warm and loose from when I'd stretched earlier. Everything feels in working order, so I lead us to the starting line.

"Not that you will," I say to Tansy, "but if your muscles start burning or you can't catch your breath enough to speak, then pull up. Stamina is easy to fix. Injuries are not."

"Fine," she says, jamming her hands on her hips.

I can tell we're on the verge of witnessing a huff.

"Then let's go," Griffin says. "I'll take the lead; Tansy, you'll run middle, and Phoebe will bring up the rear. She's used to that," he teases.

"You'd better run," I say, lunging for him.

Before I can smack him on the shoulder, he pushes into a run and starts following the little yellow flags marking our course. Tansy follows him, easily matching his gentle pace. I remember to start the stopwatch and then fall in behind her, knowing Griffin placed me here so I could watch her form . . . and her condition.

He starts off at a jog, clearly not wanting to push Tansy beyond her ability. Without having discussed a plan of attack, I know he's going to keep nudging up the pace until I let him know she's reached her peak. But halfway through the one-and-a-quarter-mile course, he's at top training speed, and Tansy is still in perfect shape. Her form is a little rough—her arms flap around a little too much and she lets her hips sway instead of keeping them in line—but she hasn't missed a step. She doesn't seem to be wearing out.

We hit a straight stretch and Griffin turns to glance back over his shoulder. Our eyes meet. He lifts his brows, silently asking me what I think. I shrug and lift mine back, indicating that everything seems good to me. Then he's facing front again and maintains his pace.

As we round the final bend of the course and the finish line comes into view, Griffin says, "We're almost there."

"Let's do another lap," Tansy says, not sounding at all out of breath.

"Phoebe?"

"Yeah," I say, suitably impressed by Tansy's endurance and willingness to work hard. Feeling confident, I suggest, "Why don't we switch to the blue course?"

"You sure?" he asks.

The blue course is the longest, measuring in at eight miles. It also has a two-mile-long section that boasts a thirty-degree incline. I've run it a few times, but always on fresh legs.

Something tells me that not only has Tansy run the blue course before, but that she's probably run back-to-back laps.

Just to make sure, I ask, "You up for it, Tansy?"

"Yes!"

"Okay," I say as we cross the finish line and turn immediately back onto the course. "Why don't you take the lead, then."

She turns and looks at me. "Really?"

I nod and before I can say, "Really," she speeds up and passes Griffin to take first position. He drops back to my side and asks, "Are you sure she's ready?"

"She thinks she is," I say, watching her pound the dirt. "She deserves a chance to prove it."

Twenty minutes later, we're racing up the incline, working hard to keep up with Tansy's pace. Her training speed is at least fifteen seconds faster than Griffin's. And a couple seconds faster than mine. By the time we reach the decline, he and I are both breathing hard and a low burn is starting in my quads. From behind, I can't tell if Tansy is wearing out. Her arms may be hanging a little lower than when we started, but I can't be sure.

We pass the seven-mile marker. Only one blessedly flat mile left.

I think our distance endurance is improving, but we need to push harder. I'm exhausted after less than ten miles and the trials are only four days away.

"The finish line," Griffin says.

I look ahead. "Thank the gods."

We're so close. For a second, I imagine myself already across the finish line, already starting my recovery. Before I can take another step, I'm surrounded by a bright glow. I blink. When I open my eyes, I'm standing at the finish line, watching Griff and Tansy run toward me.

"What the—"

"That was way cool," Tansy squeals as she crosses the finish line and pulls up to a stop.

Griffin jogs over to me. "You okay?"

"Yeah, I—" I shake my head. On instinct, I reach down and punch off the stopwatch. "I didn't mean to do that."

"I know."

"What do you think of my stamina now?" Tansy asks in between gasping breaths, like I'm not over here freaking out about accidentally using my *autoport* powers.

This is exactly what I was afraid would happen—I was so focused on crossing the finish line, on winning, that I just . . . I don't know. I bet that's the sort of thing that happened to Dad. He probably never even meant to use his powers to succeed in football. It was an accident, but he got smoted anyway.

I half expect the gods to smote me on the spot.

My legs start shaking, and not just because the muscles are

exhausted. Griffin wraps his hands around my upper arms and squeezes.

"Take a deep breath," he whispers so Tansy won't hear. "You're fine."

"But what if they—"

"They won't." He sounds so certain. Like the gods wouldn't dare contradict him. Thankful for his steady reassurance, I lean into him a little.

I nod and whisper softly, "I'm fine."

His bright blue eyes watch me, maybe making sure I'm not just saying that. I give him a tiny reassuring smile. Apparently satisfied that I've returned to my sanity, he steps back.

"I'm impressed, Tansy," he says, grabbing one wrist with the opposite hand and resting it on his head to open up his lungs.

"Ditto," I say, trying to act like everything is fine. I suppress the urge to bend over and rest my hands on my knees. That will only make it harder to breathe—and won't do anything to steady my tremulous nerves. "But maybe a little fast for a training run."

"Sorry," she says, her eyes wide. "I guess I was trying extra hard to prove myself."

"You did," I insist, trying to reassure her. "So next time we can try a non-life-threatening pace?"

"Next time?" She sounds shocked, like we would never want to run with her again after that.

Soon she'll understand that we live for this kind of torture. Like my T-shirt says, RUNNING IS A LIFESTYLE, NOT A SPORT.

"Yeah," Griffin says, dropping his arms back to his sides as he continues to cool down in little circles. "You're a better slave driver than Coach Lenny."

As we all keep circling, Tansy beams. She looks like we promised to give her a pony for Christmas—or the ancient Greek winter holiday, Brumalia.

"What was our time?" Griffin asks, his breathing returning to normal.

I look at my watch. "Sixty-two minutes!"

"Nine and a quarter miles in sixty-two minutes?" He shakes his curly head. "At that pace, we wouldn't just finish the trials, we'd *win* them."

"Amazing job, Tansy," I say, resetting my watch. Our running time disappears and the actual time flashes. "It's just after nine. We'd better finish our cooldown and head to the showers. Why don't we cool down on the track?"

We all agree, and Griffin and I grab our sweatshirts from the drinking fountain—way too heated up to put them on.

As we walk toward the stadium, I slip my arm through Griffin's. He smiles down at me and then presses a quick kiss to my nose. Everything with Griffin feels completely back to normal. Now if I could just get the rest of my life there.

❧❧❧❧❧

ORCS AND STORM TROOPERS ENTER AT YOUR OWN RISK

"Knock on the door already," Troy says.

Shaking my head—I need to stop trying to understand the descendants of Hephaestus . . . they are beyond normal comprehension—I rap twice on the door. Nothing happens.

Nicole pounds repeatedly on the smooth wooden surface. "Open up."

"Not like that," Troy says, snatching her hand away from the door. "How I showed you."

I take a deep breath and hold it. Having a secret knock is a little extreme, I think, but clearly Urian is not answering the door for anything else. Repeating the pattern Troy taught me, I finish knocking and then step back—as if the door might explode or something.

"Password?" Urian's voice is muffled by the still-closed door.

I can't bring myself to say it.

"Holy Hades," Nicole snaps. "Just let us in, Nacus."

No response.

Troy elbows me in the ribs.

I clench my jaw and grind out, "Ares wears pink underpants."

Griffin would so kill me if he heard me utter those words.

The door swings open and Urian waves us inside. I'm not sure I want to go, but Troy pushes me in ahead of him.

"What did you find out?" he asks Urian as he closes the door behind Nicole.

Urian drops into his desk chair and grabs his mouse. A few clicks later, he says, "Nothing yet. My bot is still scanning the Academy server. It's at ninety-eight percent, so it should be done soon."

"Okay then," I say, turning and trying to scoot around Troy to reach the door. "Thanks for trying. See you later."

"Not so fast." Troy grabs my shoulders before I can escape. "You have an hour until midnight. Maybe Urian's search program will find something by then." He looks me straight in the eyes with a very serious older-brother-like intensity. "Sit."

While I appreciate the whole looking-out-for-me thing, I don't need a babysitter. And I don't need to sit around in the dark when I could be staking out the courtyard or something.

"Chill, Travatas." Nicole shoves against his chest until he steps back.

"Like I said in my note," Troy says, giving Nic a narrow-eyed glare. "I'm not letting you go to the courtyard until we know who you're meeting."

"As if you could stop me," I mutter, crossing my arms over my chest. I'm starting to get annoyed. "What note? I never got a note."

"The one I tucked in your pocket while you were running this morning," he argues—not the best move at the moment. "I saw your sweatshirt hanging on the water fountain when I was on my way to your house."

"There was no note," I repeat.

Since I'm wearing the same sweatshirt I took with me this morning, I slip my hands into the pockets. Empty.

"See," I say, pulling the pockets inside out. "Empty."

"No, that's not the—"

Knock, knock, knock.

We all freeze at the loud banging on the door.

Well, most of us freeze. Nicole reaches for the handle.

"Don't move," Urian whispers, grabbing Nic by the wrist. "They'll go away."

They don't.

Knock, knock, knock. Louder this time.

Nic glares at Urian—like he is the dirt stuck to the gum attached to the bottom of her combat boot—until he releases her. Actually, his hand snaps back like she gave him a 220-volt shock. I wouldn't be surprised.

She goes for the handle.

"Nooo!" Urian shout-whispers.

But he doesn't have to stop her. Before she can reach the handle, it turns and the door flings open.

"Griffin?" I gasp. "What are you—"

"I was about to do my laundry when I found this"—he shoves a crumpled piece of paper in my face—"in my pocket."

I pull back, trying to bring the paper into focus—even though I'm pretty sure I know what it is.

"That's my note," Troy says, pointing at the paper. "How did you get it?"

Thanks, Troy. That helps.

Griffin is obviously furious. His eyes are all squinty—thankfully focused on Troy at the moment—and his full lips are clamped so tight they look outlined in white "You slipped it into the wrong pocket, genius."

"There's no need to get nasty," I say, defending Troy. It's not his fault.

Griffin's blue eyes, burning white-hot, focus on me so intently I'm not sure he even sees anything—or anyone—else in the room. You know that whole protective thing I was thankful for last night? Well, here it is again, lashing out. I try to keep calm by telling myself he's just worried about me. My getting defensive is not going to improve the situation.

"What is this about?" he demands.

Acutely aware of three pairs of very observant eyes, I slam my palms against Griffin's chest and push him out into the hallway. He and I have been through enough. We don't need an audience. "Privacy."

"Phoebe," he practically growls.

"You know I got that note pointing me to the record of my dad's trial," I point out. When he nods, I explain. "Then I got an e-mail. And another."

"How many?"

"Five, in all."

"From who?"

"I'm not sure," I say. "The sender's address was blocked."

"In your Academy e-mail? Not possible."

"Apparently it is," I insist, trying not to get annoyed that he doesn't believe me. Like I would make that up. "I couldn't get them to print, either. So we asked Urian"—I nod at the door behind us—"for help."

"What did the e-mails say?"

I explain the content, inching away as his expression grows darker with every word. He looks like he could explode at any second. By the time I finish, I'm pressed up against Urian's door.

"Why didn't you tell me about this?"

"We weren't exactly in a sharing mood the past few days," I say. "Besides, I don't see why this is such a big deal."

"I don't think you should go."

"Why not? Everyone seems so sure this is some master plot or something." Like I'm important enough for someone to master-plot against me. "What if it's just someone trying to help me out?"

Although the fire in his eyes is gone—replaced by an equally intense blank look—and he isn't moving a muscle, his entire body is practically radiating tension. If Nola were here, she'd probably tell me that his aura is fire-engine red right now. It doesn't take major deductive or psychic powers to realize he's upset. And, if it wasn't my dad we were talking about, I'd probably appreciate the concern.

"Then why all the games?" he replies. "Why not just mail you the record or leave it on your doorstep? No." He shakes his head. "This reeks of mischief."

"You're being ridiculous. 'Reeks of mischief.' What are you, a character from Shakespeare? I'm going," I say, daring him to argue. Which, of course, he does.

"No," he grinds out, "you're not."

"You can't stop me." I turn to grab the door handle, but Griffin snags it first, holding it shut.

"Yes I can," he says, sounding overly alpha male. "I will do whatever I have to do to protect you from harm."

I want to spin around and chew him a new one. To say that it's just his Hercules heroic gene that's making him so protective.

But I know that's not true—not entirely anyway. Besides, I don't like using that against him, like it's a tool I can use to win an argument.

Instead, I say softly, "You won't." I lay my hand over his on the handle. "Because you would never forgive yourself if you kept me from finding out the truth about my dad." His hand softens beneath mine, but doesn't move. "And because you're afraid I'd never forgive you, either."

His hand drops away.

Before I turn the handle and slip back into Urian's room, I say, "Thank you for trusting me."

◦◦◦◦◦

At eleven-thirty, I'm leaning against the courtyard wall, trying to stay in the shadows and keep an eye on the two entrances at the same time. All of the classrooms that overlook the courtyard are dark and only the faint glow of moonlight illuminates the smooth stone floor. The tiny pieces of the intricate mosaic at the center shine like those glow-in-the-dark jellyfish we learned about in freshman biology. I can't make out the design at the moment, but I know from memory that it depicts Plato and Athena—the cofounders of the Academy—locked in a heated debate.

I can just imagine what they're arguing about. The ideal political state. Ethics and education. Who looks better in a toga.

I stifle a snort at my own joke.

"Somehow I knew you wouldn't wait until midnight."

I spin around, face-to-face with the one person I never expected to see here.

"Damian?" I can't stop blinking. Damian isn't here. He's in Thailand with Mom. Trekking through the Southeast Asian jungle. On their honeymoon. They're not getting back for another two days. Oh no, maybe something happened. Maybe Mom—

"Your mother is fine," he assures me with a knowing smile. "She is sleeping peacefully in our Nakhon Pathom hotel room."

It still bugs me how he can read minds, but I'm more in shock over the fact that he's here. In this courtyard. Right now.

"Then what are you doing here?" I ask. "How did you know I—"

"I sent the e-mails, Phoebe." He places his hand on my shoulder. "I sent the note."

That doesn't make any sense. Why would Damian go through all this mystery and superspy subterfuge? He could have just picked up the phone—or, considering the rates to place a call from Thailand, sent a *non*blocked e-mail. Besides, he is so not the type to play games.

When he doesn't seem to be reading my mind—or at least he's not acting on what he reads—I ask, "Why? The mystery, the suspense, the secrecy. Why would you do it this way?"

"For many reasons," he replies cryptically. "The foremost of which is that I wished to distract you from your looming test. I believed that if I diverted your worry from your powers, you might more easily control them."

Ha, like that worked.

"Skepticism aside," he says. "Consider this: When was the last time your powers behaved erratically?"

"This morning," I say without hesitation. "Griffin and I were training with Tansy, and as we—"

"I know." He always seems to know way more than should be possible. It's like he's got this whole island wired or something. "*Autoporting* surprised you, but it did not misbehave. That was exactly what your subconscious was trying to achieve."

Maybe he's right. I mean, I was exhausted and desperate to get across the finish line and then, suddenly, I was. At least I hadn't zapped myself to Finland or anything. The last time my powers truly freaked out on their own was the first day of camp, when I turned Stella into a birthday cake.

His distraction had worked.

"Was that the only reason?" I ask. "Keeping my mind on something else?"

"No," he explains. "I chose the lure of your father's trial in an attempt to draw out your strongest emotions."

"Why?" I shake my head. "Everyone says emotions hijack your powers."

"Exactly."

"I don't understand."

"Phoebe, learning to control your powers is about more than passing a single test." He steps forward and places his hands on my shoulders. "For your own protection, you need to have complete mastery over your powers. Even in the face of emotional upheaval."

"Oh." I guess that makes sense. Nothing could shake me up more than anything to do with Dad. If I can control my powers in the midst of all that, then I can control them in any situation.

But does that mean it was nothing more than an emotional distraction?

I shake my head in disbelief. "So this was all some kind of mind game," I say, a wave of really uncomfortable emotion welling in my chest. "There never was anything new in my dad's trial record, was there?"

"On the contrary," Damian says, clasping his hands together in his very formal way. "There are many things in the transcripts you may wish to see."

So there really is something in the record. And he really is going to let me see it. I'm about to ask what it says when Damian steps sideways into the darkest shadows.

"But no one must see what I am about to show you, so you must send your friends away," he says, his voice a low whisper. When I look at him like he's crazy—I'm here alone, aren't I?—he adds, "A pair of them are about to burst through the far doors, and a third has been watching you from the second story chemistry classroom since shortly after you arrived."

I scowl up at the classroom window. That would be Griffin, I'm sure of it. Stalking out into the moonlight, I look directly into what I know are his bright blue eyes—just so he knows I know—and point toward the Academy entrance. I sense his hesitation and then a shadow finally moves across the darkened window and I know he's gone. Probably to go wait on the front steps.

Then, before I can even turn back to see if Damian is impressed, the far doors fling open and Troy and Urian come racing into the courtyard.

"We've got it," Troy shouts.

"My computer finished its search," Urian says, holding up a computer printout and looking extremely proud of his geeky self. "We figured out who sent the e-mail."

"Yeah," Troy gasps, skidding to a stop in front of me, "it's—"

"Damian," I say, bursting his bubble. "I know."

Urian drops his jaw. "How?"

I jerk back over my shoulder. Footsteps echo across the courtyard and I know Damian has stepped out of the shadows.

Troy—who is always kind of a chicken when it comes to authority figures—blanches. "Um, ah, Headmaster Petrolas," he stammers. "I thought, um, you were in, er, Thailand."

Damian takes two steps toward Troy, who is practically shaking, and says, "I am," in his best headmaster tone.

Troy looks too scared to speak.

"Yes, sir," Urian says, grabbing Troy by the wrist and dragging him backward across the courtyard. "You were never here. We never saw you."

Damian smiles and gives me a quick wink.

"On your way out," he says, before they disappear through the doors, "see to it that Mr. Blake remains at a safe distance."

Urian actually salutes and then pushes Troy through the doors.

I squint at Damian. "You enjoy inciting fear, don't you?"

He gives me an innocent look—which is probably where Stella learned it—and says, "It does seem to help keep the peace."

Damian definitely has hidden depths. Who would have imagined he would send me anonymous notes and e-mails and *autoport* himself all the way from Thailand just to . . . Wait, I'm not sure what he's really doing here.

"Hey, so why did you—"

"I thought you would never ask," he says with a mischievous grin.

Who is this guy, and what has he done with my stuffed-shirt stepdad?

"Follow me."

I do follow him. All the way to the center of the courtyard. He stops on the mosaic, one oxford-clad foot on either side of Plato's head.

"What I am about to show you," he says, sounding more and more into the whole spy game with every word, "you can never tell another soul. None know and none *can* know."

"You're not talking about the secret archives, are you?" I ask, remembering Mrs. Philipoulos' similar warning to me and Nicole. "Because honestly, everyone already knows about that."

"No," he says, squatting down and placing his hand on Plato's nose. "I am not speaking of the archives." He presses on one of the mosaic tiles, no bigger than a half-inch square, which slides down about an inch. "I am speaking of this."

"Of wh—"

Before I can finish my question, the ground beneath my feet starts shaking. All the tiny tiles in the mosaic quiver back and forth. My California-bred instincts kick in and my first thought is, *Earthquake!* Does Greece have earthquakes? Maybe it's a volcanic eruption, or tsunami, or—

"I suggest you take two steps back," Damian says, calm as can be. "Unless you wish to end up at the base of a very long staircase."

For half a second, I'm frozen in confusion. What is going on? Isn't this a natural disaster? What staircase?

Then, as Damian's smug look turns to concern, I heed his warning and take a giant leap back. Just as the mosaic beneath my feet drops. It falls in a series of thunks, leaving a steplike ledge with each crash. I feel like I'm in one of those Hollywood secret passages, where the movie hero pulls the gargoyle's head and a stone staircase appears in the floor.

"What the—"

"We must hurry," Damian says, stepping onto the first ledge and waving at me to follow. "The stairway will only remain open for a short time. And I need to return to your mother before she discovers I am gone."

As he moves down the stairs, I hesitate. This is so weird. I can't count the number of times I've been in this courtyard and never thought twice about this mosaic. And all the time it was a secret entrance to—

"Phoebe," Damian shouts up from the bowels of the Academy. "We do not wish to be caught below when the stairway closes. I assure you it is not a pleasant experience."

Throwing my worries and wonders to the wind, I hurry down after him.

chapter II

PHOTOMORPHOSIS
SOURCE: APOLLO

The ability to control light and fire. Most common expression consists of bringing light into an area of darkness (i.e. a cave or basement). May also manifest as fireworks, flames, and, in remarkably rare cases, fire-breathing. Do not attempt fire-breathing as it does irreparable damage to the esophagus!

DYNAMOTHEOS STUDY GUIDE © Stella Petrolas

TRAILING DAMIAN DOWN A DARK, dank corridor beneath the Academy courtyard was not where I expected to be right now. Somewhere in the back of my mind, I still thought it was going to be Stella or Adara pulling my chain. Maybe even Xander—his name was on the library employees list and he has taken somewhat of a personal interest in my problems. But Damian?

"I never would have guessed it was you," I say. "Stella or Adara, maybe. Xander even. But not you." Then again, it *is* just like him to make me work for my information.

"Keeping you guessing was part of the plan." Damian laughs, then his voice turns more serious. "Xander has explained his situation?"

"Yeah," I say. "He won't tell me what happened the year he was gone, though."

"That is at his discretion." Damian sounds a little sad. "The gods tend to make their punishments deeply personal."

I can understand that.

"Well, I feel better about the whole test thing, just knowing he went through it already and—aaack!" I squeal as I stumble over an uneven stone and pitch into the wall.

"Are you all right?" he asks from somewhere up ahead.

The faint moonlight that had illuminated the staircase and a few feet beyond faded into black about twenty steps ago. I can't see an inch in front of my face and have been following the sound of Damian's footsteps.

"I'm fine," I say, wiping my damp palm against my jeans. "I can't see anything."

"Of course," Damian says.

I hear footsteps and a soft click. Suddenly the hall is bathed in flickering torchlight—very medieval.

"My apologies. I was so focused on getting to the vault that I did not take into account that you have never been here before."

"No problem. I've taken worse tumbles in my life." Really I'm just thankful to see that the dampness on the walls is just condensation and not something more disgusting like slime or mold. "We're going to a vault?"

"Yes," Damian says, turning and continuing down the corridor. "I removed the record from the archives last fall."

"Why did you send me the call number if you knew it wasn't there?"

"Because I—"

"Wait. The distraction. I get it." I may not like it, but I get it. "So you moved it . . . ?"

"Yes. Several inquiries into Mount Olympus documents came across my desk and I grew concerned that someone might stumble upon your father's record. I moved it to the vault to protect you."

"To protect me?" I ask, practically jogging to keep up now that we can actually see where we're going.

"I didn't want you to discover the contents of the record carelessly. I wanted to present them to you myself." He pulls up his hurried pace as we reach the end of the corridor. "You were not ready to learn the truth. I now believe you are ready to make that determination for yourself."

Before I can get offended that he thought I couldn't handle the truth before—we went through all that last year with the Greek-gods-are-more-than-myth thing—I notice where we've stopped. The corridor dead-ends at a small chamber with twelve doors radiating out in a semicircle. It looks like some sort of medieval labyrinth, with walls of massive dark stone blocks and giant-size doors that look like they're made of high-rise-grade steel. Above each door, carved into a giant slab of stone that spans the entire doorway, is a very ancient-looking symbol. The symbol above each door is different.

"What are these?" I ask nervously.

"*Dodecathuron,*" he replies. "The twelve doors of Olympus."

"Of Olympus?" I repeat. "As in *Mount* Olympus? Do these doors lead there?"

Damian shakes his head. "When the Academy was built, the gods fought over the right to patronize the school. After many weeks of violent battles, Themis finally proposed a compromise. Each Olympian would be the school's patron for one month of the year. None of them was entirely happy, of course, so each demanded a separate access portal."

"But you said they don't lead to Olympus?"

"They don't," he explains. "They lead *from* Olympus. If we were to open one of the doors, we would find an empty room on the other side."

"If they're empty," I point out, "then where is the vault?"

Damian turns back toward the corridor we just left and points. "There."

"Where?" I ask, spinning back around and expecting an empty hallway. Instead, there's a giant steel door filling the entire space that we just walked through. "H-how?"

Whirling in a three-sixty, I confirm that I'm not crazy. There are the twelve doors of Olympus, the vault door, and solid stone walls. What happened to the corridor we just came down? And how are we supposed to get out?

"There is a safeguard on this room," Damian explains, stepping to the steel door and deftly spinning the combination lock above the handle. "Once someone enters the room, it shifts, turning on a smooth and silent revolve to reveal the vault."

"How is that a safeguard?" I ask.

"If someone enters who does not know the combination . . ." He sounds a little smug as he grasps the handle and twists. A loud click echoes in the chamber just before the door creaks open. ". . . they will not be able to get out."

"So what?" I ask, glancing around the room to make sure I hadn't missed spotting the skeletons of unwitting students who had been trapped here. "They would be stuck here and die of starvation—" I suddenly realize there are no air vents or anything. "Or suffocate when their oxygen runs out?"

"You should consider a career as a writer of fiction," Damian says, stepping into the massive vault and scanning over the shelves of books that line one side. "You have a very vivid imagination."

"No," I explain, stepping closer and peeking in at the vault's contents, "I've just read enough myth to know better."

Damian laughs.

The vault itself is the size of Cesca's walk-in closet—in other words: huge. As tall as the corridor ceiling, it's at least six feet wide and so deep I can't see the back wall. I am not about to step inside—I've seen enough after-school specials about kids getting accidentally locked in a safe—or maybe that was a refrigerator—to know better. But even from my position of safety, I see tons of stuff.

The entire left wall is lined with deep bookshelves, full of leather-bound books that look even older—if possible—than those in the secret archives. On the right, there are even deeper shelves, like the ones you use in your garage to organize junk. They're jam-packed with boxes and baskets and see-through storage containers. Each one seems to be carefully labeled in Greek letters, but I bet it's a nightmare to keep track of everything.

"What is all of this?" I ask absently, not really expecting Damian to answer. He's not generally the forthcoming type.

"The vault is designed to safeguard the most dangerous items of the Academy collection," he explains.

"Dangerous stuff from the library?" I ask.

"From all of our collections." He pulls a book from the stack and dusts off the cover. "Here it is."

I've been trying to translate one of the Greek labels, but when he says that my eyes instantly snap to the dust-covered leather-bound book. My heart goes crazy in my chest. Right there, in Damian's hands, is the record of my father's trial. The proceedings that led to the smoting decree—a virtual death sentence.

Damian holds it out for me.

My hands shake as I reach for the record. I'm not sure what I expect, but nothing earth-shattering happens when my fingers close over the leather. The ceiling doesn't crumble. I don't get zapped to Hades by some unforeseen curse. I don't wake up and find that it's all a dream.

I glance up at Damian, suddenly very afraid and very nervous. What if there are things in here that I don't want to know, things I can't handle?

"You do not have to read it now," Damian says, his voice soft and reassuring. "In fact, you do not have to read it at all. It is rightfully yours. You may keep it as long as you need. I know you will guard it well."

At this exact moment he's not being smug or parental or headmaster-like or anything but understanding.

Clutching the record to my chest, I say, "Thank you, Damian."

Then, before I can stop myself, I rush forward and throw one arm around him in a big hug. He doesn't even hesitate before wrapping his arms around my shoulders and hugging me back. For the first time since being uprooted and thrown into his world, I feel like we just might—*might*—become family.

Our stepdad-stepdaughter moment is cut short by a deep rumbling sound coming from the depths of the vault.

"We need to go," Damian says, abruptly releasing me and stepping back. "Now."

I barely jump out of the way before he grabs the open vault door and slams it shut. He fingers the combination lock and spins it back and forth quickly. I'm trying to figure out why he's opening the vault again when he twists the handle, and instead of the vault opening, the vault disappears. The corridor is back.

"Hurry," he says, grabbing my arm and propelling me into the hall.

With my dad's record clutched under one arm, I jog toward the distant staircase—the distant moonlight. I hear Damian's oxfords echoing on the stone floor behind me. When I reach the stairs, the ground starts to tremble again.

"Up," Damian shouts over the growing roar.

I take them two at a time, my quads screaming that they still haven't fully recovered from running the stadium steps. I burst into the courtyard and turn around in time to see Damian leap from the opening to land on Athena's feet, just as the staircase closes up behind him.

He rolls onto his back, eyes closed, and panting. With a nervous giggle, I decide not to point out that he's getting his suit dirty.

"I am most definitely getting too old for this," he says between pants.

I've never seen Damian overexert himself like this.

"Why didn't you just zap us out of there?" I ask, wishing I'd thought of that before running for my life.

"Impossible," he wheezes. "The safeguard blocks powers usage in the chamber and the corridor."

Standing over Damian, I say, "That's pretty inconvenient."

I offer him my hand.

He takes it and lets me haul him to his feet. "Inconvenient, but necessary," he says, dusting off his suit. He glances at his watch. "I need to get back to your mother. I trust your friends will see you home safely."

"Of course," I say, sad that he's leaving already. "I guess you can't tell Mom I say hello."

He smiles, like he can sense my sadness. "I'll tell her."

I give him my best smile—but I bet it comes off pretty weak.

"Is everything else all right?" he asks. "Your running. Your friends."

"Yes," I say, glad I can honestly say things with Griffin are fine now.

"And your powers?" he asks. "They are less erratic. Are you feeling more comfortable with your control?"

I bite my lip. It's not like I can lie to him—he'll read my mind and know it's not true. "It's getting better. But not perfect," I admit. "I'm still having trouble."

"You will get there," he says, laying a hand on my shoulder. "I trust in you."

"I know." And I do, really. It's not like I ever expected instantaneous control. "I'm working on it. Stella and I are working on it."

"Good." He steps back and smiles. "And stop worrying about the test. I regret ever having mentioned it."

"No, I'd rather know," I say.

Better to know the demons you face, right?

Oh gods, I hope there aren't demons. What if I have to fight monsters or gorgons or something? What if I—

"Phoebe," Damian interrupts my crazy thoughts, taking both my shoulders in his hands and looking directly into my eyes. "Stop. Worry will only impede your control. Just keep practicing and keep training. You will get there."

I take a deep breath and try for some of Nola's Zen calm.

"You'd better go," I say, thinking *calm, calm, calm* so he won't read that I'm still freaking out. "Mom will worry."

"Of course." He nods and starts to glow. Then stops and says, "Oh, and tell Miss Matios that if she returns the record she *borrowed* from the archives to my office before I return, there will be no detention."

Then he glows and is gone.

Only Damian could know that a student broke the rules from thousands of miles away. Some principals have eyes in the back of their heads . . . he has eyes *everywhere*!

225

We're lucky he never found out about the time Nicole and I switched places to take fall finals. If he knew she had taken my physics exam and that I'd taken her history test, we'd be in detention until graduation.

Griffin is pacing back and forth on the Academy steps. Troy and Urian are sitting on the top step, watching him like spectators at a tennis match. On one particularly long pass, Troy notices me in his peripheral vision.

"Phoebe!" He jumps to his feet and starts toward me. "Did you—"

Griffin shoves past him and grabs me by the shoulders. "Are you all right?"

"Of course. Didn't they tell you?"

From the dark look in his normally bright eyes, I'm going to guess no.

He twists to look back over his shoulder and practically growls, "They didn't tell me anything. Except that I had to wait out here."

"Um, I need to go," Troy says, backing down the steps. "I have class in the morning."

"Coward," I taunt.

"Right." He stumbles when he gets to the last step, tripping back in his hurry to escape Griffin's wrath. "That's me." With a gulp, he adds, "Later."

Then Troy turns and rushes around the corner of the Academy, probably heading for his dorm.

Urian, realizing that he's been left to fend for himself, says, "I'll just make sure he gets home without incident."

I cover my mouth to keep from laughing as Urian follows Troy around the corner at light speed. They clearly don't know Griffin like I do. He wouldn't hurt a fly. But—he turns his attention back on me and I'm presented with the full focus of his fury—he *is* a descendant of Ares. He does a decent god-of-war impression. If I didn't know he had the heart of a teddy bear, I might run away, too.

Instead, I laugh.

"What," he bites out, "didn't they tell me?"

"The identity of the secret e-mailer." I didn't think his eyebrows could furrow any deeper, but they do. "It was Damian."

He jerks back. "Headmaster Petrolas?"

I nod.

"Why would he send you anonymous messages? Why would he send you on a hunt for your father's record?" He's still holding on to my shoulders, but his face has softened into confusion. "And isn't he in Thailand?"

"He is," I say, answering his last question first. "It's a long story."

Shaking his head, he glances down and notices the book clutched to my chest. "You found it, then."

I look at the soft brown leather, at the slightly yellowed pages that smell faintly of dust and library—not that I sniffed them or anything. That would be a little obsessive . . . right? Contained in those pages are answers to questions I never knew I had until a few months ago.

"Have you looked inside?"

I slowly shake my head.

Griffin brushes his fingertips across my cheek. When I look up into his shining eyes, he asks, "Are you going to?"

"I—" I feel the tears line the bottom of my eyes. This should be an easy answer. Of course I want to know what really happened to my dad. Of course I want to see what made the gods decide to smote him—so I can avoid accidentally doing the same thing to myself. But when I have to actually spit out the answer, it's anything but easy. "I don't know. Should I?"

Griffin takes my hand, pressing our palms together and lacing his fingers through mine. As he leads me down the steps, he says, "I can't answer that question for you."

"I mean, I should find out what happened, right?" We step onto the lush lawn, heading toward my house. "He's my dad. I should want to know."

"Maybe," Griffin says, squeezing my hand. I melt a little as he rubs his thumb back and forth across the sensitive spot between my thumb and forefinger. "But if something inside is holding you back, then you should probably clear that up before doing something you can't undo."

"I definitely can't unlearn whatever I read in here." I wave the record in the air. "Once I know, I'll always know."

"The important question is"—he lifts our joined hands and presses mine to his lips—"... what are you really afraid of finding?"

He's right. That's the question. Why am I really holding back?

From what everyone has said about Dad's death, he knowingly

used his powers to help the Chargers win the AFC play-offs. That violates a major *hematheos* rule about using our powers for advancement in the *nothos* world. If we didn't have that rule, then *hematheos* would control the planet—which wouldn't necessarily be a bad thing, but it wouldn't be fair. He broke a rule and he was punished. That's the bottom line. Right?

But what if it isn't? What if he didn't knowingly break the rule? Or what if he hadn't been given a warning? Or what if he was forced to—

"I think . . ." I start, but my voice catches in my throat.

Griffin pulls us to a stop, tugs me into his arms, and just holds me. He doesn't say a word, doesn't press me to say anything. Just comforts me until I get my emotions under control.

"I think," I finally say around the knot in my throat, "I'm afraid to find out that he was given a choice. That the gods asked him to choose between football and—"

More tears.

Griffin rubs my back in rhythmic circles.

"What if he was forced to pick football or us?" I choke out. "And he picked football?"

"Shhh." Griffin hugs me close, smoothing his hand over my hair and trying to calm me.

"I just . . ." I stammer between sniffs. "I just don't think I could stand it if I found out he'd been given the choice, and hadn't chosen us."

"Listen to me," Griffin says against my ear. "There is nothing that says you have to read the record. Ever."

Damian said pretty much the same thing. But I feel like I should want to know. Like it shouldn't matter what I find, I should want the truth.

"Part of me wants to know. Either way. Whatever the record says, knowing is better than not knowing." My voice is muffled against Griffin's chest. "But part of me is afraid." I bite my lip. "Afraid I'll lose the memory of him. That it will be forever changed because I'll always know that I—that I wasn't as important to him as football."

"You know that isn't—"

"No, I don't," I say, my voice tinged with desperation. "He might have made a conscious decision to use his powers in football—that would be bad enough. But what if he didn't knowingly use them? That would be a million times worse."

"I don't see why you—"

"Because that would mean deep down in his soul, football came first."

And what if, deep down in *my* soul, running comes first? If my dad couldn't help breaking the rules to win, then I might do the same thing. I might wind up with the same fate.

I can't say that out loud. It's too . . . possible.

Griffin squeezes me tighter, like he can sense my thoughts. Or at least my emotions. *Psychospection* is a welcome power at times like this. I let my tears soak into his shirt. I think we both realize that nothing he could say would make this any better.

Because all I can think is *What if I have to spend the rest of my life in fear of crossing that invisible line?* That's the scariest thing of all.

chapter 12

CORPOPROMOTION

SOURCE: HERMES

The ability to use the body to its fullest extent. This power may manifest as superior stamina, extraordinary healing ability, and athletic talent. Can, depending on the hematheos heritage, result in superior physical grace, rhythm, and affinity for dance. Descendants of Hephaestus lack this power entirely.

DYNAMOTHEOS STUDY GUIDE © Stella Petrolas

"PHOEBE, WAKE UP." A voice penetrates my dream. Then the owner of the voice shakes me awake. "Dad and Valerie will be home in a few hours and you're going to be late for camp. Get up."

I try burrowing under the comforter, hoping Stella will take the hint and go away. Not that she's ever been one to take hints.

"Don't make me get the ice water," she warns.

I grunt in response.

I want to get back to my dream—in which I not only win the Pythian trials tomorrow, but also the Pythian Games *and* the Olympics . . . but all while running underwater. I know, dreams never make sense.

Besides, Stella wouldn't really—

"I warned you," she says, a split second before my comforter is jerked away and a splash of freezing water hits my forehead.

Bolting up, I shout, "Are you insane?" Wiping at the water before it can trickle down to my neck and other sensitive areas, I give her my best you'd-better-run glare. "You can give a person a heart attack doing that."

"Stop being so dramatic." She holds the still-half-full glass over me. "Now get out of bed before I dump the rest on you."

She disappears before I can even begin to think of ways to murder her and hide the body.

Well, I'm fully awake now—my dream is out of reach—so I swing myself out of bed. It wasn't the ice water that jolted me awake so much as the reminder that Mom and Damian are getting home today.

Though I could be relieved that Damian is about to be home and can help me train, I'm terrified. Even though he said it could happen at any time, I felt pretty certain the gods wouldn't spring the test on me while Damian was off the island. With his return comes the looming reminder that I'm going to be tested, and soon. Summer solstice is only days away.

As I splash water on my face, my stomach is full of butterflies. What kind of test will it be? Will I be able to figure out it's the test before I fail miserably? And what really will happen if I fail? I'm picturing me chained to a boulder while a giant eagle pecks out my liver when Stella opens the bathroom door.

"You're not even dressed," she points out.

Not willing to dignify her statement by turning around, I give her reflection a look that says, *Duh.*

"Hurry up already," she says, giving me the speed-it-up gesture. "I don't want to be late today."

Rather than point out that *she* doesn't have to be late, even if *I* am—since when does she wait for me?—I ask, "What's the rush? Why are you so excited about today?"

"No reason," she says. But I see the twinkle in her eye.

She's up to something.

"Be on the front porch in five," she says. "Or I'm zapping you to camp, dressed or not."

As if the butterflies in my stomach weren't bad enough, now they're swirling up a storm at the thought of what she has cooked up for today. I can only imagine it will end in my total embarrassment—as always.

But, since my getting zapped into the middle of camp in my smiley-face boxers would mean certain humiliation, I speed up my routine and beat Stella to the front porch by a good thirty seconds.

"Are you going to tell me what's going on?" I ask as we descend the steps and head toward school.

"I don't think so," she says. "I like keeping you on your toes."

When we pass by the turn for the front entrance, I ask, "I thought we were meeting in the courtyard today?"

"We were." She smiles cryptically. "Plans change."

We round the back of the school, where Adara and Xander are waiting. Adara looks annoyed. Xander looks . . . well, also annoyed, but that's how he always looks.

There are no little campers around.

"What's going on?" I ask nervously. One or two of the ten-year-olds are always early. "Where is everyone else?"

"They'll be here later," Stella explains. "At ten."

"At ten?" I look for my watch, only to find my wrist empty. "I thought it was ten."

"It's eight," Adara says, crossing her arms across her chest.

Spinning on Stella, I ask, "Why am I here two hours early?"

Xander, silent until now, steps forward. "This is my idea."

"We think this might help you take your powers control to the next level," Stella explains.

They are being intentionally vague and evasive. I'm immediately on guard. If this were some simple exercise, they'd just tell me without all the dramatic suspense. "What is 'this' exactly?"

No one answers.

Adara steps forward, carrying a black sash. "Trust me?"

It's only half a question. Asking me and telling me to trust her at the same time. A week ago, I would have shouted, "No way!" But ever since she shared her darkest secret, we've had a kind of understanding. She hasn't once threatened to smote me.

I turn my back, letting her secure the sash over my eyes.

"What am I supposed to do?" I ask. "Guess how many fingers you're holding up?"

"Not exactly," Xander says, moving closer and taking my elbow. He leads me . . . somewhere. All my senses are on high alert because I can't see my surroundings. I can hear the crunch of our footsteps on the gravel path.

"So . . ." I say as the scent of pine fills my nostrils. "Are you going to tell me what's going on?"

"You're going to complete an obstacle course."

"Blindfolded?" I stop in my tracks, only slightly pleased to feel Xander jerk to a stop next to me. "Are you crazy?"

I reach up to rip off the blindfold, but Xander's hands clamp around my wrists.

"Listen to me," he says, his voice low and close. "In order to tap into your powers, sometimes you have to stop relying on your senses. You don't need to see the obstacles to overcome them."

"But what if I get hurt?" An image of me sitting in the bleachers at the Pythian Games, my leg encased in a massive cast, sends a shiver through me. "The trials are tomorrow and I need to be in peak condition."

"I placed a protection on you," Stella says. "Nothing will happen to you while you're on the course."

I relax a little.

Until Adara adds, "But if you use the protection, you'll fail that obstacle."

"Fail?" My heart thumps. "Is this my test?"

"No," Xander answers. "But treat it as if it were."

I start to ask more questions, but he cuts me off. "Remember when I said I hoped you never found out the consequences of failing the test?" he asks, like I could forget. I've been stressing about it ever since. He continues, "Well, that's not exactly the truth. What I meant was I *knew* you would never find out."

"You knew?" That makes no sense. "What do you—"

"No one at school knows my heritage," he says, his voice low and right next to my ear so the girls can't hear. "Only Headmaster Petrolas knows I'm a descendant of Narcissus." He pauses, and then adds, "His son."

Whoa. That means he's even farther up the tree than I am. He makes my three degrees of separation seem like a seventh cousin thrice removed.

I remember the myth about Narcissus. He was completely infatuated with his own reflection, in love with his own perfection to the exclusion of everything else. I'm surprised Xander confided in me, but now his feelings about superficiality make a lot more sense.

"Believing he had learned his lesson on self-absorption, the gods paroled him with a grant of temporary immortality." Xander's voice wavers a little. "He met my mother. And quickly proved he had learned nothing."

For a jaded rebel boy, he sure is sharing a lot of very personal info. He must have a reason. I ask, "What does that have to do with me?"

"To make up for having to be *his* descendant," Xander explains, "and to protect me from succumbing to the same fatal flaw, the gods granted me the ability to see beneath the surface in others. I can see into a person's deepest center. Do you know what I see in you?"

I shake my head.

"A great and powerful *hematheos*," he whispers, "with a pure heart."

That heart beats a little faster.

"You will succeed, Phoebe."

Then he turns me, gives me a little push, and I know he's gone. I feel completely alone. Part of me is tempted to take off the blindfold and go home—I'm too old for games like this. But the rest of me knows that I have to do this. Solstice is days away, and after that little *autoporting* stunt I pulled in our training run, I know I need to get my powers under control once and for all.

Before something irreversible happens.

As worried as I am about the trials tomorrow, I won't be running *any* races if I'm smoted to Hades. This is more important than a single competition.

I focus my energy on my surroundings, trying to get a sense of what I have to do. I take three steps forward, then stop. An image of a fallen tree pops into my mind. I see it blocking the path, its tangled branches daring me to try climbing over. Carefully—like I'm feeling for the last step in the dark—I take a step forward.

Bending down, I feel around for what I sense is there. When my hand hits the rough bark of a pine trunk, I shriek, "It's really a fallen tree!"

No one responds, but I know they're watching.

Telekinesis flashes in my mind like a neon sign.

Great, if this obstacle tests a single power, I bet the rest of the obstacles test the rest of the powers. Thank the gods I finally studied Stella's guide.

I focus on moving the tree out of the path, on the tree already *being* out of the path. Two seconds later, I sense that it's gone.

Forcing myself to trust my instinct, I take a step forward. Then another. And another. Until I'm well past the spot where the fallen tree had blocked my path.

"How was that for perfect?" I shout to the course.

Excited by my success, I turn and move on to the next obstacle. Twenty paces into the woods, I feel a spray of water across my face. An image of flood-making heavy rain appears.

"You've got to be kidding," I mutter. When Adara tied the blindfold over my eyes five minutes ago, the sky was cloudless clear blue. Now it's pouring?

Must be obstacle number two.

Stay dry, I hear in my mind.

Okay. I hold out my hand, which promptly gets soaked in the deluge two feet in front of me. *Hydrokinesis,* I think. Control and movement of water. As I take a step forward, I focus on the water not hitting me. *I'm staying dry,* I think. *Not a molecule is going to hit me.*

Even as I move fully under the downpour, I can't feel a single drop on my skin or clothes. I hurry through the rainy section—it's like I can feel the rain sliding around me, over me, but not on me—and emerge on the far end completely dry.

"Woo-hoo," I shout to myself.

Maybe this course isn't going to be as tough as I thought.

Three steps later, the image of a sheer drop-off blares red in my mind. I pull up just inches before the edge.

"What the—?"

Mentally, I try to see over the edge. Maybe it's just a short drop and I can climb down. But I can't see anything. It's like a fog is obscuring my mental view of the bottom.

Okay, so clearly I need to get down there, wherever that is, but how? *Autoporting* is out, since I don't know where I'm going—I don't really want to end up at the core of a boulder or something. What am I supposed to do, fly?

Then I remember Nicole asking me if I flew the day I earned my *aerokinesis* merit badge. That must be the way down.

Stepping forward until the toes of my Nikes hang over the edge, I try to call up the air. My track pants whip back in the wind. It feels like a mini-hurricane is swirling around me.

I hesitate.

Afraid you can't do it? Adara's taunting voice echoes in my mind.

"Of course I can do it," I shout back above the wind. I feel like an idiot getting all defensive with a disembodied voice. Then I mutter even quieter, "I hope."

Taking the biggest leap of faith in my life—I know Stella's protection won't let me get hurt, but it's hard to make my brain fully believe—I step over the edge. Rather than plummet to the unseen depths below, I bob like a beach ball in the ocean, buoyed by a strong column of wind.

Slowly, I descend.

Halfway down I freak out. I mean, I'm floating on freakin' air. Literally. What if this isn't what I'm supposed to do? What if I'm really descending into a fiery pit or the jaws of a sea monster?

I stop descending. The air is holding me steady, not moving up or down. I'm about to send myself back up to the safety of the cliff above when I realize that my fear is the only thing holding me back. If I believe in my powers—and I've experienced them enough at this point to know that they're real—then I have to trust them.

Time to go for the gold. Taking one deep breath, I relax and let myself descend without hesitation. For three seconds, I drop through the empty air. My stomach flies up into my throat. My heart races as anticipation pounds through me.

Then I land.

Both feet touch down in perfect alignment. Sand squishes beneath my sneakers.

A beach.

I feel invincible.

Without pausing to gloat or gawk, I continue down the course until I sense the image of another cliff face. Apparently this isn't a beach, it's a gorge. And now I have to get back up the other side.

Before I can call up another wind, I hear Xander say, *Complete the puzzle.*

Puzzle? What puzzle?

There is a stack of wooden planks, each about two feet long, and a pair of long pieces of lumber with funny-shaped holes cut into them at regular intervals. I pick up one of the planks, feeling for any clues, and find that the ends of that plank are the same shape as one of the holes in either long piece. Laying the two long pieces out two feet apart, I fit the ends of the plank into the corresponding hole. When I pick up the next plank, it has a different shape at the ends, which matches up to another pair of holes in the long pieces. I click that plank into place and realize I must be building a ladder. I quickly grab the rest of the planks, locking them into their corresponding holes. When I'm done, there is only one set of holes left in the two long pieces, the uprights. I double-check that there isn't another plank lying around. Nope, I've used them all.

I lift the ladder to set it against the cliff, and it falls apart.

"Aaargh!" All my work just evaporated.

Clearly, I missed something. I quickly repeat my procedure. When I get to the point where there is just one set of holes left, I stop to think. Maybe the ladder fell apart because this set of holes was left empty. So I need to fill them, even though there aren't any more planks.

I smack myself on the forehead. How could I be so dumb? If there aren't any more planks, then I need to *neofacture* one!

Seconds later, I'm plugging the plank I created into the ladder, setting it against the cliff, and climbing to the edge above.

I totally rock.

I feel the heat one rung before I reach the top. It's scalding, like someone just opened the oven door. Ignoring the urge to climb back down, I try to get a clear picture of what I'm facing.

Flames.

I see a huge wall of flames, blocking me from climbing up onto the level surface above. Fire. That has to do with—I cling to the ladder with one hand while I wipe at my sweaty brow with the other—*photomorphosis*. Controlling light and fire.

The heat is getting worse, closer. I take a deep breath to clear my head, but my lungs fill with smoke. Fighting my instinct to shimmy back down to the gorge—or to rely on Stella's protection—I concentrate on controlling the fire.

I picture the flames shrinking, receding, backing away from the cliff's edge. Slowly, the heat fades. When I can no longer see fire in my mind, I haul myself up the ladder and dive onto the safety of solid ground.

As much as I want to lie on my back, sucking in deep, smoke-free breaths, I want to finish this course more. Climbing to my feet, I push forward.

When I reach a broad, open field, I stop. Something isn't right. Too easy. It looks like a big grassy spot, but something tickles at my brain.

I center myself, focusing all my energy on the field and what I'm not seeing in my mind. As I focus, my image changes, and I see a series of open pits, holes in the otherwise level earth.

Aha! *Visiocryption*. Someone must have cloaked the opening of the pits with an image of grass. Now that I can see the holes, I avoid them as I navigate through the field. The path ducks back into the woods and winds around until it reaches a shallow canyon with a decent-size river running through. An old, rickety rope bridge spans the canyon. It looks like an overweight butterfly could send it crashing into the current below. There's no way it will support me—even at my training weight.

There could be another way across, upriver or farther down. Even though I can't see through the sash, I turn my head as I try to see if there is a more reliable-looking bridge over the canyon. From the corner of my mental vision, I see the image of the bridge flicker. The rickety-looking version fades and a far more substantial wooden bridge appears in its place.

When I turn back, I see the rickety bridge again. Someone must have cloaked it, too. I reach forward, expecting to feel the solid bridge under my fingers. Instead, I feel fraying rope.

The sturdy bridge must have been altered, not cloaked. *Visiomutated.*

It only takes a second to reverse the *visiomutation,* and then I'm scurrying across the bridge.

I'm starting to think nothing can surprise me. Until I turn a corner and sense Stella, Adara, and Xander blocking my path.

"What?" I ask. "Did I do something wrong? I didn't use the protection."

Why else would they be here?

When they don't answer, I say. "Okay, guys. If I haven't screwed up, then get out of my way so I can finish."

They just stand there, immobile and silent. Maybe this is some kind of mental mirage. But when I reach forward, half expecting my hand to go right through Stella, my palm hits her shoulder.

"What?" I ask, louder this time. As if maybe they didn't hear me.

Nothing. Absolute silence.

But there is something about the looks I'm sensing on their faces, like they're concentrating really hard, that makes me think I'm missing something. I can practically feel Stella's gray eyes burn into mine, and not in her favorite I'd-smote-you-if-I-could way. It's like she's trying to tell me something.

What on earth is she trying to say? I stare right back at her. Maybe if I concentrate hard enough I can read her—

Choose.

I hear the word as clearly as if she'd said it out loud. Only, she hasn't spoken—not out loud or in my head. This was *outside* my head, if that makes any sense.

She smiles, like she's glad I figured it out. Figured what out? Choose. What on earth does that mean?

I turn to Adara, like she might have answers. She's still concentrating. I try my trick again, of staring back at her and concentrating—

Door.

I definitely heard that. And it was definitely outside my head. Maybe I really did read their minds.

Duh! *Psychospection.*

I turn my attention on Xander and read his thought.

Three.

Choose. Door. Three.

Choose door three?

Before I can ask any questions, Stella, Adara, and Xander shimmer away. Apparently I cleared that obstacle.

Around another corner, I find the answer to my question. There are three doors—very *Alice in Wonderland*—each with a big gold number on the front.

"Door number three, then," I mutter to myself as I pull the door open.

As soon as I step through the door, I can't move. I'm frozen mid-step. It's like someone turned on a freeze machine, but my brain doesn't know it's supposed to be frozen. I can still think and hear and see my surroundings, but I feel like someone shut off all my muscles.

Help, I try to scream. But I can't open my mouth. No sound vibrates in my throat. I can't call out for help.

I start to panic. My heart is beating faster than it ever has. Tears well in my eyes.

Help, I try again. *Help, help, help.*

That's not working. Maybe someone is still close by, watching out for me. Maybe they'll see that I chose the wrong door—or whatever sent me into this trap—and come save me.

After what feels like several torturous hours—but was probably like two minutes—I realize no one is coming. Stella and her posse aren't going to rescue me. I can't scream to let them know I'm in trouble.

There has to be another way.

If they can't hear my voice, maybe they can hear my mind.

Help, I say with my mind. I focus my mental communication, my *psychodictation,* on Stella because I know her best. That might make my efforts easier. *Please,* I beg. *Help. I'm trapped. Set me free.*

Instantly, I'm free and stumbling forward onto my hands and knees.

All you had to do was ask, Stella replies.

"Aaargh!" I scream at no one. I should have known it was just another obstacle.

I take a minute, allowing my heart rate and adrenaline levels to return to the vicinity of normal, before moving on. Right now I just want this stupid obstacle course done.

I tear ahead, focused on finishing to the exclusion of everything else. I almost don't see the barricade of briar bushes until it's too late. At the last second, their image flashes into my mind—thanks to self-preserving *corpoprotection*, probably. I don't have time to do anything but react. Instinct and some *corpopromotion* superstrength send me high-jumping over the barricade, and landing safely on the other side.

"For the love of Nike," I grumble. "How many times do I have to almost die or get seriously injured?"

Okay, I have to admit that, even without using the protection, I haven't actually *gotten* injured. And maybe, just maybe, that's part of the exercise.

Deciding that caution is more important than speed, I set out at a walk. I try to mentally list the obstacles I've done so far. If you count the briar barricade for two powers, then I've completed eleven. Eleven (dangerous) obstacles without injury. My powers haven't failed me once, guiding me over, around, and through as if my eyes were wide open. Better, even. If I could see what I had to face, I'd probably be too scared to attempt it.

Considering the twelve *dynamotheos* powers, I expect just one more obstacle. No big deal. I'm in the homestretch.

When I round a bend in the course and find myself up against a solid wall, I stop in my tracks.

In my mind I can see the wall perfectly. It's tall, maybe ten or twelve feet, spans the entire width of the path and into the woods beyond, and is completely smooth. Focusing my powers, I search for a foothold or a rope or anything that will get me over. Nothing. It might as well be a wall of ice.

Maybe my mental image is wrong. Maybe it's not as tall as I think.

I walk forward until I'm about a foot away, bend down, and jump as high as I can, reaching for a ledge to grab onto.

My body smacks full-on into the wall. As I slide back down to the ground, I wonder how on earth I'm supposed to get over this obstacle.

"You can't defeat this obstacle so easily," Stella says from somewhere to my left. "Even if we removed the blindfold, you couldn't succeed through physical means alone."

"This is the ultimate test," Adara adds. "You can only get through by using your powers."

What on earth does that mean? Before I can ask them to explain, I feel a soft breeze and know that they're gone.

Okay. I can figure this out. I've made it this far trusting nothing but my powers—and my sense of self-preservation. Surely getting over a wall can't be that hard.

"It's not about going *over* the wall," a distant-yet-familiar voice whispers within my mind. "Feel the victory inside you, Phoebester."

Dad?

That is *not* possible. I give my head a brain-rattling shake. I must be suffering from sensory deprivation after being blindfolded so long. My subconscious is playing tricks on me. That's all.

"Come on," Adara shouts from the far side of the wall. "We have to start camp soon. I'd hate to leave you out here on the course."

She grunts, like someone just elbowed her in the gut.

"We believe in you, Phoebe," Stella says. "You just have to believe in yourself."

I roll my eyes behind the blindfold. As if that's not a cheesy, movie-of-the-week line. Still, I want to finish this course. To prove that I can handle anything they throw at me—the counselors *and* the gods.

"Okay," I say to myself. "Think this through. If there's no way *around* the wall. And I'm not about to make it *over* the wall. Then there's only one other option . . ."

Suddenly I know exactly what I have to do.

I managed it that night on the beach, when my emotions took the reins, and on the cross-country course the other day. Now I just need to use my mind to achieve the same result consciously.

Placing my palms to the wall, I picture myself on the other side. I focus all my energy on having gotten myself *through* the expanse of two-by-fours. My mind shuts out all other stimuli. No sounds, no touches, no tastes, no smells. Just me, on the other side of this wall.

The hairs on the back of my neck stand up.

Someone's arms wrap around me.

"You did it!" Stella shouts. "Omigods, you were so awesome!"

I reach up and rip off the blindfold. Sure enough, I'm on the other side of the wall, at the end of the obstacle course. Stella's hugging me and shouting. Adara crosses her arms over her chest and smiles smugly. As if she's the reason I made it through. Xander is clapping and smiling.

"We knew you would make it, Phoebola."

Twisting out of Stella's embrace, I turn to find Mom and Damian standing off to the side. Looking as proud as I've ever seen them.

I run into Mom's arms. "You're not supposed to get home until tonight."

"When Damian told me what they were going to put you through this morning," she says, squeezing me close, "I insisted we catch an earlier flight so we could be here to share in your triumph."

She sounds so certain, like there was never a doubt that I would make it through this obstacle course. I was never that sure.

"I'm glad you're here," I whisper.

As she tucks a loose clump of hair behind my ear, she says, "It killed me to be so far away while you were struggling." She smiles painfully. "But you're such a strong, independent girl, I knew you needed to process this on your own."

"I know." Besides, it's not like she could have helped me or anything. This is kind of beyond the realm of her psychoanalytical expertise. And if I'd really needed her, she would have skipped out on her honeymoon in a flash.

I hug her a little tighter.

"Come on," Damian says, clapping a hand to my shoulder. "Let's go celebrate. I think you can skip camp for today."

Emotions are boiling through me. I can't believe I made it through the whole course blindfolded. I can't believe I *autoported* through the wall. But most of all, I can't believe I heard Dad's voice in my head.

eeeee

After everyone has gone to bed, I sit down at my desk and power up my laptop. While I'm waiting, I dig into my pocket and pull out the merit badges Stella gave me after dinner. I pin them onto the bulletin board above my desk, next to the ones I've already earned. A dozen little badges of honor. I'm still getting used to the idea that my powers might actually be under control.

The beeping and whirring stops and I click open my IM. I don't really expect my girls to be online—it's crazy early in L.A. and I have no idea if Cesca even has Internet access in Paris—but amazingly enough, the smiley faces next to both their user names are bright yellow.

Cesca starts chatting before I can even say hello.

PrincessCesca: about time!

LostPhoebe: hi!!!

PrincessCesca: I only have a few

PrincessCesca: have to meet François in twenty

LostPhoebe: François?

GranolaGrrl: new French bf

LostPhoebe: you've only been there like a week!

PrincessCesca: not my bf

PrincessCesca: but he is deliciously yummy

I can't help laughing. Leave it to Cesca to find a hot French boy-friend in record time. She never seems to have trouble attracting a guy—she just never seems to want to hold onto them for very long. Maybe this one will be different.

GranolaGrrl: speaking of bfs . . . what happened with yours?

LostPhoebe: we're totally back together

LostPhoebe: I can't believe I thought he was cheating on me

PrincessCesca: wait, what? you and G broke up?

LostPhoebe: only for a weekend

GranolaGrrl: I don't believe in saying I told you so

GranolaGrrl: but I told you so!

LostPhoebe: I know

PrincessCesca: a girl makes one little trip to France and all hell breaks loose

I can just picture Cesca, crossing her arms over her chest and pursing her perfectly glossed lips in annoyance. It's been too long since I've seen her and Nola.

LostPhoebe: any updates on visiting Serfopoula?

PrincessCesca: my sched is pretty busy

PrincessCesca: but I can always sneak away for a weekend

GranolaGrrl: the grant committee met

For several long, torturous seconds I stare at the blinking cursor. Waiting. Hoping. Waiting. It's not like Nola to make us sweat like this.

LostPhoebe: and . . . ???

PrincessCesca: dish already, envirofreak

PrincessCesca: I got a hot date

GranolaGrrl: I

GranolaGrrl: won't

GranolaGrrl: be

GranolaGrrl: there

My heart dips into my stomach. I know it was a long shot, but I was so counting on her coming, so looking forward to her visit.

PrincessCesca: damn

GranolaGrrl: until August!!!

LostPhoebe: omigods, yay!!!

PrincessCesca: well played, bi'atch

GranolaGrrl: you two can't have all the fun ☺

PrincessCesca: gotta run

PrincessCesca: e-me the dates and I'll be there

PrincessCesca: luck in your race tomorrow P

LostPheobe: thx Cesca

LostPhoebe: have fun with François

PrincessCesca: always XOXO

GranolaGrrl: night

Cesca's smiley face goes blank. I'm always sad to say good-bye, but this time I'm more excited about them coming to the island at the end of the summer.

LostPhoebe: you know the Pythian Games are in August

LostPhoebe: if I make the team you guys can come

GranolaGrrl: of course you'll make the team

GranolaGrrl: *victory* is assured <wink>

I smile at Nola's Nike joke. Even though Damian let me tell my girls about the whole descendant-of-the-gods thing, we're still not supposed to chat about it online. He's convinced someone is going to intercept the transmission and spill the *hematheos* secret to the world.

He's way paranoid, but I do *not* want to be on his bad side.

GranolaGrrl: I'm glad things worked out with Griffin

GranolaGrrl: he's your perfect match

LostPhoebe: I think so too

GranolaGrrl: you better get to bed

LostPhoebe: yeah, gotta get up early

LostPhoebe: love you

GranolaGrrl: love you!

We sign off and I shut down the computer. I give the merit badges one last look before I tuck in. For the first time since Damian told me about the test, I'm feeling pretty confident. All I have to do is get through tomorrow's trials and then everything will be cake.

"Ground my powers."

Griffin rolls his eyes at me. "I am not grounding your powers," he says. "Even if I could, I wouldn't. You can control them on your own now."

I'm not so sure. I mean, yeah, I completed the obstacle course yesterday with flying colors, but that's because I was totally concentrating. I didn't have anything else on my mind. Like, say, the *freakin' Pythian Games trials*!

This is the biggest race of my life, so I might be a little distracted.

"Please," I beg. "Just for this race. Just to make sure I don't . . . accidentally use them."

"You won't." He presses his lips to mine. "Besides, I told you, I *can't.*"

"But what if—"

"I know you're worried about accidentally using your powers," he says. That's the understatement of the millennium. "I've been thinking about what you said about your dad's record. How you're afraid to read it."

The record has been sitting under my bed ever since I got home from meeting Damian in the courtyard that night. Every time I catch a glimpse, it's like it's taunting me. Tempting me to face my fears. But I'm far too chicken.

"First of all," he says, "I never knew your dad, but I can't imagine a parent that selfish could have raised such an amazingly compassionate daughter."

I give him a half smile, because I think he's definitely overstating my compassion. After the way I've treated him and overreacted in the past, I think I'm currently pretty low on the compassion scale.

"And second," he says, oblivious to my unspoken self-deprecation. "I want you to consider this: Would *you* give up the people you love for a cross-country win?"

"Of course not!" How could he even think that? "I would never—"

Griffin holds up a hand to stop me. "That's my point," he says. "I've never known anyone who loved their sport as much as you. If you wouldn't make that choice, I can't imagine your father would."

My rant deflates. He's right. I love running more than almost anything. But only almost. I don't love it more than Mom or Griffin—or, on a good day, Damian and Stella. Dad *must* have loved us more than football.

"You're right," I say slowly, smiling. "I don't think he chose football over me and Mom consciously or otherwise."

My insides are calm—maybe for the first time in a long time. When Dad died, I remember being so very angry. At him, at Mom, at whatever deity or act of nature had taken him from us. At myself, too, for the possibility that I'd taken him for granted while he was alive. Then, when I found out that he was *hematheos*, that he was smoted for that, the anger had returned. Maybe I didn't even recognize it, but it was there. Bubbling under everything.

Griffin made me see what I couldn't—that the anger had come from fear.

Now, even though nothing has changed except my perspective on the situation, the anger is gone.

Maybe I'll even read the record—someday. It suddenly doesn't seem like such an important decision. I know and love and trust my dad. I don't need to read a trial transcript to know that.

"Good," Griffin says, tugging me to his chest and slipping his arms around my waist. "Because you have a race to run, and you won't win if you don't focus. And if you don't make the team, Coach Lenny will blame me. He'll probably make me run to Beijing and back."

I love that my overactive imagination is rubbing off on him.

"Racers to the starting block," Coach Lenny's voice booms through the megaphone, "for the women's long-distance trial."

Griffin gives me a squeeze and a shove in the direction of the race.

My heart rate quadruples. People in the *nothos* world may not have ever heard of the Pythian Games, but in this world they're the equivalent of the Olympics. Making the Cycladian team, competing against the best *hematheos* racers in the islands, is not going to be a cakewalk.

When I step into the starting box, though, my anxiety disappears. This is my home turf—literally, since we're racing on the Academy course, but also figuratively. Distance running is my world, *hematheos* or not.

Coach Lenny lifts the starting pistol into the air and fires.

I turn on the autopilot, taking off with the two dozen other women competing for the three precious spots on the team. They're all strangers, mostly older than me and from other islands in the Cyclades. There was no planning and strategizing how to beat the other racers ahead of time. This is just me, running my race. Five laps around the five-mile white course plus one around the yellow.

Tuning out everything but my feet and the course ahead, I run.

By the time I finish the fifth white lap, I can't feel my legs. My lungs burn fire with every breath. I don't know how long I've been running, but it must be over two hours. The end of my pain is just a mile and a quarter away.

As I make the turn from the white course onto the yellow, I begin to take stock of my surroundings. Not the trees and bushes and woodland critters; the other racers. There aren't any.

Although I can't see them anymore, I know there are two racers ahead of me on the track. Through my pain, I'd absently taken note when the two blondes had pushed out from the lead group a couple miles back.

I risk a glance back over my shoulder. I don't see any racers behind me, either, but I can hear their footbeats on the path.

The anticipation of victory eases my pain. Third place means a spot on the team, and right now that's all that matters to me.

When I face back to the front, there is a racer on the course. Her long brown ponytail bounces with every step, obscuring the competitor number pinned to her shirt. I blink my eyes, certain that I'm seeing things. She wasn't there a second ago. But, no matter how many times I squeeze my lids shut and reopen them, she's still there.

She also isn't one of the two blondes who'd pulled into the lead. That means I'm in fourth place. There are no prizes for fourth.

"Impossible," I mutter between gasping breaths.

Then, realizing the futility of denial, I turn off my shock. She is only about ten paces ahead of me. I can catch up with her on this final lap—maybe not easily, with my legs feeling al dente, but I can do it. When it comes to running, I can do anything.

Drawing on every last ounce of my energy, I increase my pace.

She must sense my acceleration, because she speeds up identically and keeps her solid lead.

I try again.

She matches me again.

Three times I speed up, only to watch her lead stay constant.

Finally, when I know I have next to nothing left to give, she starts pulling away. I'm getting left behind and there's nothing I can do. Tears of frustration sting my eyes. I was so close—*so close*—to making the team, but my body just doesn't have the juice to catch her.

We round the final bend in the yellow course, onto the straightaway to the finish line, and I watch her twelve-pace lead extend to thirteen. Fourteen.

"Aaargh!" I scream at myself. "Do something!"

My body responds by sending a shooting pain up my spine.

It's so unfair. I *owned* this race. I deserve a place on the team.

But even as I rant in my mind, I know the truth. No one *deserves* to win. You have to earn the honor. And clearly the racer in front of me earned that honor today.

I focus my gaze on the finish line, intent on finishing this race with the pride that a fourth-place finish deserves. Maybe I can learn from this racer, from this loss. I'll become a better athlete—

"What the—?"

In an instant, the girl with the long brown ponytail disappears. Not she-crossed-the-finish-line-and-disappeared-from-sight. Just . . . vanished. She glanced back over her shoulder, gave me what looked like a wink, and then evaporated. In a puff of smoke. Well, that was different.

Seconds later, I'm across the finish line. Coach Lenny is the first to rush me, grabbing me around the waist and lifting my dying body into the air.

"I knew you'd make the team, Castro," he screams. Then, to the crowd, "This is my girl!"

"But . . . but . . ." I'm too exhausted to form the simple, burning question.

Coach Lenny drops me, nearly sending me to my knees, to record the time of the next racers to cross the finish line.

"Congratulations, Phoebola," Mom says, hurrying to my side and placing supportive hands on my hips.

Doubled over in utter exhaustion, I manage to twist my head enough to glance up. Griffin is there, beaming at my victory. And Damian looks like he just won the lottery.

"Yes, congratulations," he says, unable to hide a grin beneath his stuffy exterior. "You just passed your test."

"What?" I gasp.

"That was your test," he says.

"My what?" I manage to pull myself vertical. "My test? You mean that racer . . ."

"She was no competitor. Actually," he says, clearing his throat. Leaning close, he whispers in my ear, "that was Nike."

My jaw drops and I am incapable of speech.

"Despite your drive to win," Damian explains, "you did not use your powers."

"So that was it?" I ask. "Not cheating was my test?"

"No," he says. "Proving that you and not your emotions master your powers was the test. It was not about honor—even the gods cannot regulate a person's honor—but about mastery. You did *not* want to cheat even more than you *did* want to win."

I can't believe it. I passed my test! Even as Griffin steps past Mom to wrap me in his arms, whispering congratulations in my ear, I can't believe I just passed the test . . . by losing to *Nike*!

"Racers to the starting block," Coach Lenny calls out again, "for the men's long-distance trial."

I release Griffin and shove him toward the box, like he'd done for me.

While he's jockeying for position with the other racers, I take my place in front of the spectator section, prepared to cheer him on at every lap.

"He's going to win, you know," Adara says as she slides up next to me.

"For once," I reply, giving her a grin and a sideways glance, "I think I'm actually going to agree with you."

"Someone call the *Chronicle*." She stifles a fake yawn. "This is headline news."

Coach Lenny fires the starter pistol into the air. As the guys take off to follow the same course I've just run, I break out in a grin. Next to me, Adara eyes me warily, as if I might seek revenge for her months of torture, now that I've got my powers under control.

Now that I *trust* myself to control them.

With all the people I care most about in the world—yes, even Stella (who is here *with* Xander!)—gathered around to cheer my victory, and Nola and Cesca just an e-mail away, I can't help thinking I'm a pretty lucky girl. I've got my powers under control. I'm going to be racing in the Pythian Games. I just ran on the same course as my goddess ancestor. And—although I could never prove it and I'd deny the insane idea if anyone suggested it—I have a feeling that Dad was right there by my side with every step.

Out of all the moments in my life, this is the most perfect.

I sling an arm around Adara, ignoring how she cringes away. She has nothing to worry about from me. We goddesses have to stick together, you know.

EPILOGUE

"ARE YOU READY?"

I look up at Griffin standing in the doorway to my room. He looks so yummy in his tracksuit—turquoise blue with baby-blue stripes, the colors of the Cycladian team—with his sunglasses perched on his head. The Pythian Games racecourse at Delphi isn't wooded like the Academy course, so we're definitely going to need the shades.

"Almost," I say, grabbing my Nikes from under my desk and dropping onto my bed to pull them on. "I just need to lace up."

"Your mom and Headmaster Petrolas are waiting at the dock." He walks over to my desk and picks up the framed picture of us running on the beach. He's smiling when he says, "I think they're more nervous than either of us."

I finish lacing one Nike and move onto the other. "Well, it's not every day their daughter and her boyfriend get to race in ancient mythological games that used to be as big as the Olympics."

As I finish my bow, I catch sight of the leather-bound book under my bed. For luck, I run my fingertips along the smooth spine. Over the gilded letters of my dad's name.

"Have you read it yet?" Griffin asks, his voice a soft whisper.

"Not yet," I say, sitting up and snatching my turquoise duffel off the floor. "Let's go."

Griffin offers me his hand and I take it, loving the way his palm feels hot against mine. I also love that he doesn't press me about the record. It's not that I'm afraid to read it—we got past that weeks ago. I'm not sure how to explain it except that I haven't *needed* to read it yet. Someday I will, I know. One day something will happen or I'll just wake up knowing that the time has come to find out the whole truth.

But for now, I'm pretty content as is.

"So after we win the Pythian Games," Griffin asks as we head to my door, "what next? The Athens marathon? The Olympics? The Oxford cross-country team?"

As I turn to pull my bedroom door shut, I see the record poking out from beneath my bed.

"Yes. Yes. And—" I point at the record. It glows for a second and then slides out of view. "Yes."

Griffin laughs out loud. Wrapping an arm around my shoulder, he says, "That's what I love most about you. You always set attainable goals."

I know he's teasing. Because if I've learned one thing in the last year, it's that *anything* is attainable.

After all, I *am* a goddess.

SOME MYTHS ABOUT ACKNOWLEDGMENTS

1. *Don't thank the same people twice.* So not true. Thank you again . . . Sarah Shumway, for editing this book through tough times on both our sides—and for only sending one revision letter this time, even if it was longer. . . . Jenny Bent, for your unapologetic honesty—I appreciate it, really I do—and for the good news phone calls, even if you never let me share the news. . . . Sharie Kohler, for being my cheerleader, sounding board, and coconspirator—and for making me a part of your family, even if I'm never sure whether that's a blessing or a curse. (Just kidding. It's a blessing. Always.)

2. *Only thank friends you see on a regular basis.* If that were true, I couldn't thank Kay Cassidy (for agreeing to read the rough draft—even though it spoiled the ending of *Oh. My. Gods.* for her) and Stephanie Hale (for being my online snark sister—even though I'm secretly afraid of being the object of said snark) because I don't want to live where they live.

3. *Don't thank fans.* Whatever. Why else do I write these books? Thank you everyone who read and loved *Oh. My. Gods.*, and took the time to let me know—especially Kirsty, since you'll always be my very first fan.

4. *Thanking bookstores is kissing up.* It probably is. I don't care. I have to thank the amazing ladies of Blue Willow Bookshop for the most amazing debut party in literary history—or at least in *my* literary history.

5. *Only total dorks thank their parents.* Okay, that one is true. But I'm going to do it anyway. Thank you, Mom and Dad. For everything.